The
Somerset
Tsunami

Emma Carroll

90 YEARS OF EXCELLENCE
FABER & FABER

First published in 2019
by Faber & Faber Limited
Bloomsbury House,
74–77 Great Russell Street,
London WC1B 3DA

Typeset in Garamond Premier by MRules
Printed by CPI Group (UK) Ltd, Croydon CR0 4YY

A CIP record for this book
is available from the British Library

ISBN 978-0-571-33281-6

FSC
www.fsc.org
MIX
Paper from
responsible sources
FSC® C020471

2 4 6 8 10 9 7 5 3 1

PRAISE FOR

'Emma just gets better and better and BETTER.'
Scott Evans, *The Reader Teacher* & #PrimarySchoolBookClub

'A remarkable writer.'
Daily Mail

'Perfect for captivating the imagination.'
Mumsnet

'Absorbing... brimming with atmospheric detail.'
Carousel

'My go-to author for historical fiction.'
Bookbag

'Rich in thrilling details.'
Lovereading4kids

'Compelling storytelling.'
BookTrust

'Fast, exciting.'
School Librarian

'If your middle grade kids (ages 8-12) haven't discovered
Emma Carroll yet, then they're missing out.'
Irish Times

FABER & FABER

has published children's books since 1929. Some of our very first publications included *Old Possum's Book of Practical Cats* by T. S. Eliot, starring the now world-famous Macavity, and *The Iron Man* by Ted Hughes. Our catalogue at the time said that 'it is by reading such books that children learn the difference between the shoddy and the genuine'. We still believe in the power of reading to transform children's lives.

About the Author

Emma Carroll was a secondary school English teacher before leaving to write full time. She has also worked as a news reporter, an avocado picker and the person who punches holes into Filofax paper. She graduated with distinction from Bath Spa University's MA in Writing For Young People and is now an award-winning and bestselling author. *The Somerset Tsunami* is Emma's tenth novel. She lives in the Somerset hills with her husband and two terriers.

For Alice, word witch

Person for TRIAL

On suspicion of
WITCHCRAFT

TO BE HELD AT THE
SPRING ASSIZES

GLASTONBURY,
FOR THE COUNTY OF SOMERSET

12th January 1616

1

A FEW MONTHS EARLIER …

IN WHICH OUR HERO'S LIFE
TAKES A STRANGE AND
DRAMATIC TWIST

1

We lived in a hamlet called Fair Maidens Lane, which wasn't a lane at all, but half a dozen moss-roofed cottages cowering against the weather. For as long as I could remember, there'd been no grown men amongst us, just women, girls and my brother, Jem. As for fair maidens, there was Abigail, my elder sister, though she was only middling pretty. Our womenfolk were a capable lot, breeding pigs, catching fish, crushing herbs, and birthing babies in the local towns and villages, and had a reputation for doing all of it well. Yet we were our own little community, bounded by the Severn Sea on one side, the Quantock Hills on the other. And because none of us needed rescuing like maidens in stories had you believe, our hamlet's name came to be a fine joke. No harm was meant by it, at least, not then.

The first sign of change was a slight shift in the air which I supposed was the coming of autumn because it made gooseflesh rise up along my arms. Then Jem, who at fifteen summers was two years my elder, got taller as if he'd grown overnight like a magic plant. Every morning his breeches rose further from his knees. Where once he'd been as soft as a fresh loaf, he was now all wrist bones and shoulder blades, and had a voice that squeak-boomed when he spoke.

'Mercy, brother! Grow any taller and the birds'll start perching on you,' I exclaimed one morning when he had to bend to avoid the ceiling beam above our heads.

'Come here and say that, Fortune Sharpe!' he threatened, Fortune being my name, though I was yet to discover why.

We chased each other out of the house, ducking and squealing under Abigail's laundry lines, which sent next door's youngster pigs tottering to the fence to see what all the fuss was about. Our neighbour, Saddleback Sally, was known far and wide for breeding exceptional pigs. We ran on, past Leathery Gwen's, who had skin as tough as hide from the hours she spent catching crayfish along the shore. The timber cottage opposite hers was home to Ruth and Jane Redfern, local midwives and clever in the ways of herbs.

Before we knew it, we'd reached the last dwelling in the hamlet, Old Margaret's, with its dairy where she made delicious yellow cheeses. In the pasture beyond, she kept a herd of cows that our mother, and her milking stool, tended every day. Mother was paid well for her skill. And so we'd always been told to be polite to Old Margaret.

As Jem and I hurtled past, still laughing and shouting, Old Margaret was out in her yard rinsing cheesecloths.

'What's all this noise, then?' she cried, flapping a cloth at me. 'Anyone would think the devil himself was chasing you!'

I slowed down.

'Haven't you anything more useful to do than tear around, making mischief?' she scolded.

'Sorry,' I muttered, though I'd never been a walk-on-tippy-toes sort of girl, and Old Margaret knew it as well as anyone. I'd grown up wearing boys' shirts and leggings, and my only dress was an ugly hop-sack thing that'd once been Abigail's. Unless Mother told me to wear it, it stayed stuffed in a dusty corner under my bed.

Old Margaret turned to Jem. 'About time you earned your keep, and all.'

'Yes, mistress, sorry, mistress,' he said, so contrite I couldn't help sniggering behind my hand.

Apologising again, we hurried on. A sharp left took

us up over the common land before it dropped away steeply to the coast. If you followed your feet downhill through the gorse bushes, you'd arrive at a little brown-sand cove where the river ran into the Severn Sea. It was my favourite place in the whole world – not that I'd seen much of anywhere beyond Bridgwater, but still.

The beach was empty. Once Jem and I had wrestled each other to the ground, and I'd declared myself the winner, we fell apart to sit on the sand. Every day I'd find a reason to come down here, to stare at the ocean and smell the salt air. It came from Father, my special love of the sea. I'd been only two years old when a savage winter tide snatched him from the shore where he'd been out glatting for big, fat eels. My one memory of him was how he slept at night with the shutters open in all weathers, just to hear the waves. It brought peace, so he'd said.

Usually, it worked like a salve for me too, yet today I found myself mulling over our encounter with Old Margaret.

'D'you think she meant it?' I asked Jem, chewing the frayed edges of my thumbnails. 'About us needing to be more useful?'

At home, us children all had our tasks: collecting firewood, feeding hens, chopping herbs, growing vegetables, making candles. Though none of it brought in any real coin, like the saddleback pigs or Old Margaret's cheese.

Jem stretched his long spindly legs. 'You know there are people watching us, don't you?'

'Where?' I spun round, scanning the hill of common land we'd just passed over.

'Not *right now*, you goose,' Jem tutted. 'Generally, I mean. It's been going on for a while, so Abigail says. They're riding as far as the crossroads once, maybe twice a day.'

The crossroads was about a quarter of a mile from Old Margaret's house. It was where the main road stopped and became a narrow track down to our cottages.

'Who's watching us?' I wanted to know.

'Our neighbouring landowners, apparently—'

'Who own all the land between us and kingdom come,' I finished for him. 'What do they want with us?'

'They're just looking – for now.'

This last bit he said in a wary, loaded way. For we both knew how rich these landowners were, and that wealth meant power. These men decided the laws a magistrate might enforce, and the punishments for breaking them.

Not that we'd done anything wrong. No one here owed money or had thieved anything or done a murder, as far as I knew. Yet the thought of being watched unsettled me. Since Jem didn't say any more about it, and with the sea spread before me, I soon forgot it, though. And I wondered how the waves might look to someone in Spain, say, or even further away in that brand-new country they were calling America. There were many different ways of seeing the same thing.

As we soon found out to our peril.

2

A few days later we were sent to collect kindling. Luckily, there'd been a high wind in the night that had shaken the trees, so the ground was strewn with dead leaves and gnarly grey twigs. It wasn't long before our baskets were full. We were about to turn for home when Jem cried, 'Tree down!' and we saw first the upturned roots, then the trunk of an oak that'd fallen right across the path.

It was pretty early in the autumn for a storm to bring a whole tree down, though it was a young oak of middling height rather than the great old ones that grew along the boundary with the pasture beyond. That said, it was a usable piece of wood. And by the looks of things, we were the first to find it.

'You know what this would be grand for, don't you?' I asked as we both stared at the tree.

'The stove?'

'This isn't kindling, flea-brain!' I was thinking fast. 'This could be a boat.'

'Who in Fair Maidens Lane needs one of those?' Jem asked.

'Anyone? Everyone?' I threw my arms up, excited. 'Think how useful a boat could be! People could go fishing in it or travel along the coast when the roads are bad in winter.'

Jem wrinkled his nose. It was a look I knew all too well, and it meant he was impressed. He'd obviously not forgotten Old Margaret's scolding, either, and could see the potential in my plan.

'We'd better hide it, then,' he said. 'Just in case anyone takes it for firewood.'

A fair bit of huffing and grunting, and it was obvious we weren't strong enough to move the tree from the path. So we made do with heaping leaves over the top of it, and hoped that would be enough to keep it hidden until we could return.

We were back within the hour, having pleased Mother enough to be allowed a little time to ourselves. I'd smuggled the short axe from the woodpile up my sleeve, and Jem's pocket bulged with his knife and a couple of razor-sharp flints. Together we set to work on our felled tree, first removing the roots and the upper branches, until we were left with the trunk itself. This alone was hard enough work, and soon we were too warm for jerkins and jackets, and sweating like a pair of pigs.

'It's going to be magic, isn't it?' Jem chattered on as we worked.

'You could wager my life on it,' I agreed. 'Everyone'll be amazed when they realise we've made a boat all by ourselves. The whole hamlet will want to use it.'

'We shouldn't tell anyone, though, should we? Not until it's done.'

'Definitely not.'

We spat on our palms and shook hands to seal the secret. Just as Jem started cutting again, his knife went still.

I sat back on my haunches. 'What's the ...?'

He told me to shush. He'd seen something – somebody – straight ahead, coming out of Old Margaret's cottage, the outline of which was just visible through the trees.

At first it was hard to see what was happening. There seemed to be two or maybe three men, all dressed in tall dark hats, their cloaks flapping about like wings. Old Margaret was in the midst of them – at least, I guessed the bare, white, kicking legs were hers. They were dragging her away, forcing her into the back of a cart. I couldn't hear what she was saying, but it sounded shrill and angry, and I'd the sudden queasy feeling things weren't right. I scrambled to my feet, thinking we should do something to help her.

It was then I saw the others: Leathery Gwen, the Redfern sisters, Abigail, all standing by, watching from the roadside. No one was interfering. Or speaking up. They were letting these men take Old Margaret away, which confused me even more.

The voice I heard next was our mother's. Milking stool still under her arm, she came charging out of the yard after the cart, shouting at the top of her lungs.

'Have pity!' she cried. 'Margaret Ford is an old woman! She is innocent of all your charges!'

Charges? I turned to Jem in amazement. 'She's not a criminal!'

Within moments, it was all over. Old Margaret was in the cart. One of the men, his hand flat on Mother's chest, shoved her out of the way. The horses strained, the cartwheels rolled through the mud, and Old Margaret disappeared from the village. Everyone else went back to their houses.

We rushed home to find Mother already there, white-faced and dazed. Abigail was trying to make her sit down, which she was refusing to do.

'Who were those men?' I asked, then realised I knew

the answer. 'Oh Lord, they're the ones who've been watching from the crossroads, aren't they?'

'You'd better tell her, Mother,' Abigail muttered under her breath. 'She'll only keep on until you do.'

Mother swallowed, wincing as if her throat hurt. 'A rival cheesemaker has made some *accusations* against Old Margaret, that's what.'

I frowned. 'Accusations?'

'Of cursing his cheese, though the man's a complete lubberwort for saying it. 'Tis his own doing if his rennet won't set, not poor Margaret's.'

'It all goes back to King James himself, so I've heard,' Abigail piped up. 'And how his mind runs to witchcraft.'

'Old Margaret's not a *witch*!' I was stunned.

'She's old and grumpy,' Jem said. Mother glared at him. 'Which wasn't a crime last time I checked,' he added hastily.

I expected Mother to tell us to stop gossiping, but all she did was give her face a weary rub.

'It's those landowners behind it,' she admitted now. 'They've always been suspicious of us. They've seen how well we live here, how quietly, and all they want is our land for themselves.'

'But it's Old Margaret's land mostly,' I said. When

the nearby monastery was abandoned its lands were divided up. Old Margaret bought a share which included Fair Maidens Lane and ran all the way down to the sea. Everyone in our hamlet rented their furlongs direct from her. It was an unusual arrangement, not least because there were no men involved.

'They can't just take it off her,' Jem pointed out.

'They can if she's broken the law – and believe me, they'll think of something. They've been jumping at the chance to get their hands on our pasture,' Mother replied.

'Why can't they leave us alone? We've done nothing wrong,' I insisted.

'We're women thriving by ourselves – that's what we've done wrong,' Mother said, and fiercely. 'If we want to survive, our life here is going to have to change.'

I was pretty certain it already had.

3

Old Margaret didn't return, despite Mother telling us she surely would. The days passed, the weather cooled, the leaves on the trees turned golden, yet we remained watchful. The landowners would be back – everyone expected it. Jane Redfern said we should block the path, Leathery Gwen suggested fresh crabs as a peace offering. No one could agree on what to do.

The very next Sunday Mother dragged us to church, making doubly sure we were tidy and that I, for once, was wearing my gown. Though the law fined people who didn't go to church, no one had ever checked on our tiny parish – at least, not in the past. Things were different now, and the sight that greeted me proved it: everyone in attendance in their best clothes, singing loudly at the hymns. I couldn't shake the feeling that it was fear that brought us here.

In the days and weeks that followed, shadows as dark as bruises grew under Mother's eyes. And when she wasn't trying to coax milk from Old Margaret's cows, she was reminding Jem and me to keep our heads down.

'You stay out of trouble, d'you hear?' she warned. 'Those landowners are looking for something to pin on us.'

'Won't Old Margaret ever come back?' I asked.

'She will, I'm sure of it,' Mother said firmly. 'That's why we're keeping her cows going.'

She'd roped us into helping at the dairy, and it was hot, stinky work. My brother, as always, was eager to please. But I wasn't easy-natured like him, or sensible like Abigail, and was soon fed up of washing pans and rinsing cloths. Since Old Margaret's disappearance, there'd been little time for boatbuilding, and we'd had to snatch odd moments before the light failed at the end of the day.

Then, another change.

People started being suspiciously nice to Jem – people who, as far back as I could remember, had chided us for our silliness and noise. Leathery Gwen offered him the pick of her crayfish catch, Saddleback Sally wanted his advice on her sows. Jane Redfern wondered if he'd like her father's best cloak? In our hamlet of bonnets and muddy skirts, my lanky brother was suddenly a prince.

I thought it funny to begin with. 'But you snore like a pig, and your feet smell of old cheese, Jem Sharpe!'

And he laughed, because he was baffled by it too – embarrassed, even.

The special treatment went on, day after day, and with it came new responsibilities. Jem was asked to check fences, weigh pigs for market, talk money with local merchants, plan services at our church. Rents were paid to him instead of Old Margaret, and he locked all the coins away in a battered box, which was then hidden in Old Margaret's cellar.

All this began to nibble away at the brother I held so dear. As if the joy was leaking out of him and he was turning into a middle-aged man. It was typical of Jem to do his best at whatever task he faced. But he no longer had time for building our boat. And I got annoyed.

We'd carved out the trunk enough for us both to sit inside it, and shaped the underneath into a sort of hull. A few more hours' work, and our little dugout boat would be ready to take down to the beach for testing in the water.

Yet on the very afternoon we'd agreed to do the finishing touches, I found Jem at the kitchen table, practising writing his name. I stood over him, impatient.

'What about our boat?' I asked. 'Aren't you coming to finish it?'

'Can't you see I'm busy?' he replied, not looking up.

'You're turning into a right dullard, you are.' I scowled at the top of his head.

Jem put down his pen and sighed.

'Now don't fly into a temper, Fortune,' he said. 'I didn't ask for this to happen. But everyone decided it would be best to have a male in charge, at least while those landowners are still sniffing about . . .'

'Balderdash!' I cried. 'The women here are more than capable, you know they are!'

Even so, a little voice chimed in my head. The world beyond our hamlet was a different place, with different rules. I'd seen it myself sometimes at market, when traders would ignore Abigail to deal instead with Jem. Then there was what Mother said, about keeping our heads down. After what had happened to Old Margaret maybe now wasn't a good time to be different.

Jem picked up his pen again. He looked fidgety and pale.

'I mean it. I'm not enjoying this any more than you are. Ask Mother if you don't believe me,' he said.

*

I'd planned to. Yet that night, noticing the frostiness between us, Mother explained before I had a chance to ask.

'It seems those men in black cloaks have lost interest in us at last.'

It was true we'd not seen the landowners again since the day they took Old Margaret.

'Having a young man to keep us in check seems to have worked,' Mother said, though from the look on her face I wasn't sure *she* agreed. 'I'm sorry it fell to you, Jem, but you were our obvious choice.'

'He's our only choice,' I remarked.

'And don't think I'm enjoying it,' Jem muttered again.

'Tsk. You've taken to it well, son.' Mother ruffled his hair, frowning as she did so. 'Though, by my word, these aren't the locks of an important young man. It's time you had your first haircut.'

Whilst she got to work on Jem's curls, I sat on the stool opposite, pulling faces. Both Abigail and Mother wore their yellow hair in long neat plaits, whereas Jem and I had the same dark knotty curls that swarmed about our heads like bees. Slice by slice Jem's locks fell to the floor. By the time Mother had finished, the difference was startling.

'You're the dead spit of Father!' Abigail gasped, hands cupping her cheeks.

'Oh Lord, he is,' Mother agreed.

Frustratingly, I couldn't remember what our father had looked like. But this serious young man with his long thin face definitely didn't look like me any more, and I felt bewildered, almost scared. It was as if I'd just said farewell to my dearest friend, and a part of myself in the bargain.

'Cut mine too,' I insisted, suddenly.

Mother hesitated. Girls didn't have haircuts: they plaited and combed their hair, or tucked it neatly under a bonnet.

'It couldn't look any worse,' Abigail reasoned helpfully.

'Just to the chin, then,' Mother relented.

A few cuts and it was done. Though I liked smoothing it behind my ears and feeling the air on my neck, it didn't make me resemble Jem again. If anything, we now both looked like strangers.

4

I finished the boat alone. I was determined to do it: with Jem proving how responsible he was, I was resolved to show I could be too. Though it didn't stop me nearly exploding with excitement. For days, I couldn't sleep right, couldn't concentrate. My brain was a whirl of boatbuilding and sea-sailing, and how far along the coast we'd travel.

Finally, when the boat was ready, I went to find Jem. It was a Sunday, after church. Jem was outside, feeding our chickens. The weather had turned savagely cold these past weeks, and he'd taken to wearing old Mr Redfern's cloak, which made him look even more unlike himself.

'The boat's finished. You coming to try it out?' I asked, praying he'd say yes. I couldn't remember the last time we'd laughed and had fun together.

Jem looked at me, eyebrows pinched. 'On a Sunday?'

The day of rest. Not just hymns in church, but

spending the whole day quietly, refraining from all but essential work. Our hamlet observed the rule more and more nowadays, but it still surprised me to hear it from my brother.

'It's not work,' I pointed out. 'It'll be a test of sorts. An investigation.'

He thought about it – a bit too long for my liking, but I tried to be patient.

'Very well,' he said, finally. 'As long as we don't go further out than waist-deep.'

Personally, I'd hoped we'd go along the coast a way. But he'd agreed to come so I was glad. And he was, of course, being sensible: of the two of us, I was the better swimmer, though neither of us was exactly good at it.

'Promise,' I answered. 'We'll just see if it floats.'

He nodded, emptying the remains of his pail amongst the chickens. The little smile on his face made my heart go skywards.

The boat was where it always was, hidden under leaves and moss. Neither of us had tried moving it again since the first time, and once we'd swept the coverings aside, I was struck by how big and solid it looked – still like a tree trunk, really, despite my best efforts. The makeshift oars I'd fashioned out of twigs didn't look up to the job, either.

'I hope it works,' I muttered, in a sudden rush of worry. There were so many things that could go wrong, and I was now imagining them, all at once.

Jem rubbed his hands purposefully. 'Only one way to find out.'

With a fair bit of grunting we half dragged, half carried our boat out of the woods and along the path to the beach. Thankfully the only living things to see us were the cows grazing on the common, their heads swinging up to watch as we staggered past.

'Bet they think we're mad,' I observed.

'Maybe we are,' Jem replied, which didn't exactly calm my nerves. Yet he was in good fettle, whistling under his breath, and his cheery mood quickly rubbed off on me.

The boat *would* float. Jem *would* be impressed. The sun was shining, the frost almost melted. And the sea – oh, the sea! – was a beautiful pale green, and as flat as a griddle pan. I felt ready to burst. Finally, we were going to sea in our boat!

The second our bare toes touched sand, Jem began walking faster – running, almost, which was no mean feat with such a heavy load.

'Slow down!' I laughed, struggling to hold on to my end of the boat.

He didn't, of course, and nor did I. We charged into the breaking waves, the cold of it making me catch my breath. The little carved-out space where we were meant to sit quickly filled with seawater. As fast as we scooped it out with cupped hands, it came in again.

We were still in the breakers, that was the problem, where any boat – even a vast sailing ship – would be bobbing like a cork.

'We need to go further out!' I yelled.

Jem's enthusiasm began to cool. 'We agreed not to go too deep . . .'

But we had to, for the boat to float. Before Jem could stop me I'd clambered on board, pushing aside the oars. The boat tipped so dangerously I was sure the whole thing was going to flip over. Just in time it steadied itself, with me crouched down, gripping the sides.

'I'm floating!' I cried. 'Oh, Jem! Look!'

'I'm looking!'

Not wanting to be left behind, he tried to scramble up beside me. The whole boat lurched again. I braced myself, ready to be pitched out into the water, yet somehow, sodden and panting, Jem managed to swing his legs up on to the boat.

'Sit down!' I insisted.

He crouched opposite me, his knees crushed against

24

mine. The wood was digging into my hips, the small of my back. We were jammed in tight, trembling with cold. Yet the boat was floating. And it kept on floating with us on board.

'Well, you did it,' Jem said, a smile spreading across his face. 'You made a boat.'

I grinned back, a little dazzled.

'*We* did,' I corrected. 'You helped me.'

He laughed. Shivered. Laughed some more. And all the gloom and nasty, knotty worries of the past few weeks seemed to shrink inside my head. With the sun on our cheeks and the sea breeze stiffening our wet clothes, I felt that sense of peace Father had spoken of seeping into my bones.

Then, like he'd plucked it from the air, Jem said, 'You're so much cleverer than me, Fortune.'

I was taken aback. 'You're the blessed child of Fair Maidens Lane, not me!'

'But I truly don't want to be. It should be Mother or you or Abigail instead,' he said, and went silent in that thoughtful, scrunched-up-face way of his.

I was almost sorry for him, then, and patted his knee clumsily, which made the boat rock. Life in Fair Maidens Lane used to be simple. As long as we did our work and didn't bleed to death or set fire to anything, we were pretty much left to ourselves. Now it was as if we had an unseen master standing over us, making sure we all behaved.

'Shall we paddle a bit?' I said, keen to shake off a return of the gloom.

I realised then I'd lost my oar, which in truth was little more than a bundle of twigs. Luckily, Jem still had his tucked down beside him.

'We'll have to take it in turns,' he said.

'Five rows each?' I suggested. 'Otherwise we'll go round in circles.'

Jem paddled first, then handed the oar to me. It didn't do much other than make a splash, and I added it to the fast-growing list of things in the boat I needed to improve on.

Yet the fact of the matter was we were floating. We were at sea. I'd done something useful, and it felt bright and brilliant.

'Perhaps next time we could try it with a little sail,' I chattered on, passing the oar back to Jem. 'Here, take it.'

But he was gripping the sides of the boat.

'Fortune,' he said quietly. 'Have you seen how far out we are? This water certainly *isn't* waist-deep.'

5

Despite what Jem thought afterwards, I'd not done it on purpose. When I started paying attention to where we were, the wind and tide had already nudged us into deeper water. The sea beneath us no longer looked green: it was a dark inky-blue. All I felt of the shore-bound waves was a little lift, then a dip. It was as peaceful and gentle as a lullaby. Had it been just me, I'd have stayed out here forever, but Jem was sitting opposite me, sweating.

'You promised to only go waist-deep,' he muttered.

'Don't fret. We're only a little way off course.'

'Yes, with one oar and a leaky boat.'

I thought Jem was overreacting, rather, and it was on the tip of my tongue to tell him to stop being so lily-livered. But when I saw just how far from the shore we were, I grew uneasy myself. The beach had shrunk to a narrow sandy strip, the hill of common land beyond a green blur, dotted with cows. We'd come a decent sixty yards or more into open sea. Away from the shelter of the cove, the wind was picking up, pushing us further out.

'Right,' I said briskly. 'Let go of the sides. I need you to help.'

Thrusting the oar at him, I leaned over the opposite side of the boat, using my hands to scull the water. A few minutes of it and my arms burned with the effort. Then we swapped over – Jem using his hands, me with the oar. It was exhausting, and Jem wouldn't lean out far, but it seemed to work. We made slow, faltering progress back towards land.

By the time we reached the breakers, Jem already had one leg out of the boat. He jumped down into the shallows, before turning on me.

'You promised we'd not go too far!' he cried, his fear turning to temper. 'What on earth were you thinking, when we can barely swim!'

'But we made it back, brother, so calm yourself,' I replied, grinning. 'We rowed a boat! You and me! We did it, together!'

He shook his head. 'You're reckless, you are! You never think things through. You just do them and expect me to follow on behind.'

That pulled me up short.

'I thought you *liked* us doing things together,' I replied. 'I thought going out in the boat would be fun.'

'If we'd stuck to the shallow water, maybe. But we could've drowned!'

'It'll be better next time with two oars, honest it will,' I tried to convince him.

Jem scrunched up his shirt hem, wringing the water from it. 'There won't be a next time! I'm not going anywhere in a boat with you again, so don't—' He stopped, mid-rant, staring towards the top of the beach. 'Who's that? Up there, look!'

A figure was standing at the place where the river ran across the rocks before soaking into the sand. My first thought was: *Mother!* Her warning about making trouble was still fresh in my ears.

It wasn't her.

It wasn't a woman, even, but a round-bellied man in a black cloak that blew sideways in the wind. On his head was a tall dark hat. The last time I'd seen a man dressed like that was when Old Margaret was taken.

Two children, fooling about in a home-made boat. On a Sunday. We were in big trouble.

There was no point in running when we'd been so squarely caught. Nor did my legs have an ounce of strength left in them. I felt suddenly close to tears. Yet by the time we'd dragged the boat ashore, the man had vanished.

'We'd better go home,' Jem said miserably.

Though we left the boat where it was, our quarrel came with us. Thankfully, Mother and Abigail were out when we arrived, so we could at least swap our clothes for dry ones before Mother's questioning began.

'What are you two fighting about?' She demanded, the moment she returned.

With Jem writing at one end of the room, and me whittling wood at the other, it was clear as day we'd had cross words.

'Ask her, she's the fool,' Jem snapped.

'Well?' Mother turned to me, hands on hips. 'What have you done now?'

I bit my lip, on the brink of tears again. I'd wanted to do something useful for the hamlet, and for Jem and me to have fun together like we used to, that was all. But saying so would make me cry and then I'd be like Abigail, who regularly sobbed her way out of trouble.

Instead, I pushed the damp hair off my face and said, as proud as I could, 'We made a dugout boat and took it to sea, and it almost worked.'

Jem spluttered. 'We almost perished, more like.'

'You got scared, that was the problem,' I pointed out.

'And you didn't get scared in the slightest. You didn't even think we might drown!'

It was true, I hadn't. But Jem was making me feel like a halfwit and it angered me.

'Just because I'm braver than you,' I retorted. 'Imagine it – a girl with more courage than the Great Leader of our hamlet!'

'That'll do, Fortune,' Mother warned.

I picked up my whittling again, my hands shaking. It took a lot for me to lose my temper, but I'd truly had enough.

'Tell Mother who saw us down on the beach – go on,' Jem goaded. 'Then we'll see how brave you are.'

Mother looked between us, frowning. 'Who saw you?'

I put down my knife. I might as well tell her: she'd only wheedle it out of me in the end.

'A man,' I said. 'In a cloak, wearing a black hat. He was watching us from up on the cliff.'

Mother went very still. 'What did I tell you about keeping out of mischief?'

I could see her panic and felt it rise up in me too. The boat, the risk we'd taken was one line we'd crossed: this went beyond it. For the man was one of those landowners and he'd seen us breaking the Sabbath.

'I know we're in trouble, so punish us and get it over with,' I said.

But it was Jem Mother turned on. 'Stop bickering with your sister and start acting like the young man you are! I demand it!'

Jem reddened. He opened his mouth to speak, then thought better of it and went out instead, slamming the door behind him.

I stayed in my seat, whittling, for the rest of the day. Yet for all the harsh words and sour tempers that thundered in my brain, I kept thinking about the boat. Jem was right: I hadn't been scared. Out there on the sea, I'd felt as if I belonged. There would be a next time: I'd make sure of it.

6

Just a few hours later, Mother woke me in the dead of night. The lamp hovering above the bed looked like a fiery evening sun. I was certain I was dreaming. All the more confusing was that Mother's voice sounded so real: 'Get up! Get dressed! Keep quiet!'

Our cottage had one big upstairs room under the eaves where we all slept – me and Jem in our little truckle beds, Mother and Abigail on the horsehair mattress they shared.

I'd gone to bed early that evening, still sore with Jem, and he with me. We'd never slept on an argument before, and now everything felt off-kilter and strange. I rolled over, burying my face in the blankets, hoping Mother would go away.

She didn't.

'Quickly now, child!' she whispered. 'We're going on a journey.'

At that, my eyes flew open. I sat up, which let the cold in under the covers.

'Where are we going?' I asked.

Mother put a finger to her lips to stop my questions, then threw me my beloved jerkin, leggings and shirt.

'Just you, mind. Don't disturb the others,' she said, which made me more intrigued because it was clear I'd been singled out. 'Meet me outside.'

Once she'd gone, I slid out from under the covers and dressed, carefully so as not to wake anyone. Jem's short hair stuck out above the blankets. Though I still felt hurt and angry with him, it was all mixed up with love.

'Sleep well, brother,' I whispered.

Jem didn't stir. Abigail looked fast asleep, yet I was pretty sure she was watching me as I went down the stairs.

*

Outside, Mother hurried me up the track towards the crossroads. As my eyes grew used to the darkness, I saw the familiar shapes of trees, bushes, then the sharp swing right as we turned inland. With the sea behind us now, we headed uphill towards Nether Stowey, the nearest town, which was where we often went for market day.

'I'm not in trouble still, am I?' I asked warily, for

I supposed Mother's curious behaviour must have something to do with the boat.

'No, you daft girl,' she replied, but not crossly. 'Now stop asking questions.'

Worried she might wish she'd chosen another of her children instead, I kept quiet.

We walked briskly. It was a bitter night, the frost sharp, the stars hard. All memories of my warm bed had long gone: I was wide awake, shivering with energy and desperate to know what this was all about. Were we meeting someone? Buying something? About to smuggle Old Margaret out of gaol?

A couple of chained-up dogs barked when we hit the outskirts of Nether Stowey, but as we followed the main road down the hill, the town slumbered on around us. Everything looked different at night – the pretty church like a dark castle, the bakery a mere barn, and the marketplace, usually buzzing with people, bleak and empty as our footsteps echoed off the stones.

Once we'd left town behind and were on the open road again, Mother finally stopped. Her face was all shadows in the starlight.

'Now then, Fortune, let's have a look at you.' She eyed me critically. 'You're skinny, flat-chested, short-haired, coarse-mannered. Yes, you'll make a convincing enough boy.'

I stared at her in surprise.

'Why's that a good thing, suddenly?' I asked. At home it was a constant battle to make me wear skirts, though I never actually wanted to *be* a boy. It was more that I didn't see myself as the sort of girl who did sewing and kept her mouth shut and wanted only to find a husband. This new thinking from Mother made me suspicious.

'Where *are* we going?' I asked again.

'Didn't I tell you not to make a fuss?'

'I'm n—'

'No questions, remember?' She took my arm.

We started walking. The trouble was, by now, I was so full of questions I had to press my lips together to stop them flying out. Mother, sensing a rebellion, kept me moving – and moving fast.

*

After another few miles downhill, the land flattened into the moors. Every winter they flooded: it was something to do with the land being low-lying and the boggy peat that lay beneath, only that night the cold was so fierce it'd turned the floods to ice. Ahead of us, the frozen fields glowed temptingly in the starlight.

'Is it thick enough to walk across?' I asked, hoping it was. I'd never seen the moors like this before and was eager for a closer look.

Mother was more cautious. 'We'd best stick to the banks. Don't want you falling through the ice and getting a chill.'

So we clambered up on to the willow banks that ran above the fields. The air smelled not of mud or silt like usual, but of a cold that made my head ache. It was as if the whole world was different, not just Mother and me, and it made me feel jittery and restless.

Mother, meanwhile, kept stopping, finger to her lips. She was sure she could hear something. All I caught were the owls and the rooks roosting in the trees above our heads.

She flapped her hand. 'Shhh! Listen!'

This time I heard it too – the faint thud of hoof beats.

Quick as lightning, Mother pulled a parcel from inside her shawl, urging me to take it. The package was small, wrapped in sackcloth. I didn't recognise any part of it.

'It's yours,' she insisted, thrusting it at me. 'For your travels.'

Confused, I didn't take it. 'But you haven't said where we're going.'

'To Bridgwater,' she replied, not meeting my eye. 'To the hiring fair.'

My jaw dropped to the ground.

'You're not thinking of hiring *me* out, are you?' I gasped.

'I know it doesn't sound much of a plan,' Mother answered quickly. 'But what with Jem having his responsibilities now and you finding that hard ... it'll be good for you to make your own way in the world ... and besides, we could always do with the extra coin ...'

'No, Mother, please!' I interrupted. The hiring fair was like a cattle market, only it wasn't beasts that were bought and sold, but people. I'd gone once with Abigail, and it was a horrid, bustling place, full of housekeepers inspecting people's teeth.

'I'm too young!' I begged. 'Take me home!'

But Mother was listening for the hoof beats, not to me. They were louder now. The thud-thud of a fast trot.

'Quick!' she hissed. 'Keep walking! Don't wait for me. If you pretend to be a boy, you'll get decent work and better pay.'

I was too stunned to move. She'd never mentioned money being short before. Since Old Margaret left there'd been more work at the dairy than we could manage: some days there'd been so much milk left we'd had to pour it into the ground.

Mother, I realised, was lying. This was about the boat. About me and Jem, and the landowner man seeing us.

'But I've argued with Jem!' I cried, tears in my eyes. 'It'll be ages before I see him again!'

Mother froze. The rider was so close now, I heard creaking leather, the snort of the horse.

'Drat it!' Mother cursed. 'Get down in the ditch.'

I gulped. The ditch in question, running alongside the path, was a drop down of two yards or more. At the bottom of it, the ice looked as hard as marble.

'As soon as it's safe to run, get yourself as far from here as you can.' Mother pressed the parcel at me again. 'Goodbye, daughter, and go well.'

But it felt too final, a parting gift for someone who wouldn't be home again for a very long time.

'I don't want it,' I said.

'Take it!' She was fierce again. 'Get gone or I'll fetch my boot to you!'

She pushed me so hard I stumbled. My feet slipped. I went crashing through brambles, then too much thin air, landing with a wallop in the ditch below.

None of me seemed broken, thankfully. By the time I sat up, the horse had stopped in front of my mother. Shuffling into a crouch, I peered through the tangle of tree roots, at eye level with Mother's worn-down clogs. The man jumped from his horse. He was wearing long leather boots with spurs on them. He barked at Mother to keep still.

Then came the terrible *sshhhh* of a sword leaving its sheath.

My heart beat so fast I thought I was going to faint. But I shifted closer, and made myself keep watching. If this man was about to kill our mother, then I had to see who the scoundrel was.

7

The thistle motif on his cape told me the man was someone loyal to our Scottish king. He wasn't a landowner but a soldier who, judging by the size of his weapon, meant business.

'Beg all you like,' the soldier sneered. 'My orders are to question any suspicious-looking women, and I'd say you fit that description, wouldn't you?'

'Let me pass,' Mother pleaded. 'I'm a decent Somerset woman. I mean no harm.'

The soldier shifted his weight. 'Then you'll know about the folks practising magic round here, won't you? Little nests of witches popping up everywhere, so the king's been told.'

I kept absolutely still. The sword hung in the air, directly above Mother's upturned face. A mere swipe and her nose would be cleaved right to the bone.

'I have no truck with magic,' Mother said, and

scrabbled in her pocket. I wished to heavens she'd keep still. 'I carry no herbs or—'

The sword came down so fast, I had to shut my eyes.

'Keep your hands where I can see them!' the soldier barked.

When I dared look again, the blade was resting on the bridge of Mother's nose. A thin line of blood trickled down her face. I'd been holding my breath.

'The king is wrong, is he?' The man laughed. 'Because there's a woman in Ilchester gaol swearing she's cursed every cheesemaker in the land.'

I knew who he was talking about and felt sick. Somehow, Mother kept her shock in check.

'I'm sure the king knows his subjects better than I,' Mother replied meekly. 'Now, if you please, I'm on my way from the cider house and I'm expected home,' and for added effect gave a little tipsy hiccup. It was pretty impressive, all told.

'Where's home?' the soldier demanded, not moving an inch.

'Fair Maidens Lane, eight miles hence.' Mother's eyes flicked in the direction from which we'd come.

'*That* nest of strange women? Where the cheese-curser lived?'

If anything, in that moment, the sword pressed

harder, the blood on her face trickling faster. I fought to hold in a scream.

'Times have changed. We've seen the error of our ways, sir,' Mother said, so calm it astonished me. 'A *Master* Sharpe now presides over us. We pays our rent to him, see, and he speaks for us at market and so on.'

The soldier grunted his approval. Finally, he lowered his sword, and I let out a long breath of relief. He grabbed Mother roughly by the shawl, heaving her to her feet, then spun her round till she was facing the way back to our hamlet.

'Go home,' he instructed. 'Where Master Sharpe can keep you safe from harm.'

Mother set off immediately without a backward glance, her shoulders hunched against the cold. I watched her go, a lump in my throat. The soldier's gaze didn't leave her, either, till she was almost out of sight. Then, satisfied, he mounted his horse again and turned in the opposite direction. Moments later, he too was gone.

I stood up with care. My legs were numb from crouching in the ditch, my thundering heart only just slowing. All around me the moors lay starlit and silent, as if nothing had happened, as if I'd dreamed the soldier and his bloodied sword, threatening my mother.

Yet the love I had for her felt very real. How she could've knelt there and not quaked in fear, I'd never know, but it strengthened me, somehow. I was the daughter of a strong woman. I could make my way in the world. If she wanted me to go to the hiring fair, then I would, and I'd make her proud. Though I didn't know quite yet what path I might take, I did at least know the way to Bridgwater.

Slowly, just in case someone was out there still, I inched along the ditch. There was ice underfoot. Brambles everywhere that snared my hair and jacket. And that cold, heavy silence covered everything like snow. Deciding it was safe to risk it, I scrambled out of the ditch up on to the bank. And there, caught between the bare fronds of a willow, was the package Mother had tried to give me.

Intrigued, I took hold of it. It was tied with a leather thong and was the size and shape of a small person's fist. It would hardly have been eye-catching in broad daylight, though out here under the stars, the sackcloth wrapping seemed an enticing silver. When I gave it a little squeeze, it felt as soft and light as air.

To be clear, Mother wasn't the gift-giving kind, and yet she'd definitely wanted me to have this. I untied the thong and parted the cloth.

Inside was – well, I didn't know exactly *what* it was. It looked like skin, or dried-out innards. A sheep's bladder maybe, a thin slice of lung, yet when I braved a quick sniff all I got was the mustiness of sackcloth. I had no idea why Mother was so insistent that I have it. Or why she was so certain it was mine.

But it was something from home, at the very least. Stuffing it inside my shirt, I took a very big breath for courage, and started walking.

*

It was daybreak by the time I reached Bridgwater. The last hiring fair of the year was always exceptionally busy. People came from miles around to buy what they needed and sell what they didn't, before retreating to their firesides for the rest of the winter. Already the town was lively with carts, dogs, horses, barrels and huge-eyed children begging for a crust or a coin. It filled me with a keen sense of purpose. I'd be all right, just so long as I didn't dwell on my parting quarrel with Jem. Or that niggling sense that Mother had been lying about why I'd needed to find work.

Joining the crowds, I made my way down to the river where the heart of the fair was held. There'd be stalls along the riverbank selling cakes, bread, chops, apples, cheese – you could buy anything and everything, if you'd money. Me, I didn't have a single penny and, after a night of walking, was hungry enough to eat a cartful of capons. It didn't help that I was following a pie-seller, whose steaming wares smelled like heaven and made my stomach growl something monstrous.

An incredible sight lay before me as I reached the riverbank. Just like the floodwater on the moors, the river had frozen over, only here people were walking on it, tottering from bank to bank as if it was nothing more than a slippery street. Almost the entire fair had shifted on to the ice. Row upon row of stalls, including ones I'd never seen before: lace-sellers, spice merchants, musicians, a dancing dog, someone offering to paint likenesses for the price of a mug of beer. I couldn't imagine how the ice was holding everything up, but I was sure as anything going to find out.

Except there was a girl in my way, dithering. She was on the arm of an extremely tall gentleman – her father, I supposed, since both were dressed in matching dark blue velvet. I was about to dodge past them both when I heard her ask, 'Won't everything sink if the ice cracks? Won't we drown, and horribly too?'

I thought it wisest to wait for his answer.

8

'The river has been freezing up for weeks, my dear,' the man replied. 'It is perfectly safe.'

'I am not convinced it *is*, Papa,' the girl kept on.

She was probably a year or two older than me, with mouse-brown ringlets and the smooth skin of someone who spent her days indoors. If Abigail were here, she'd have been sighing over the girl's wide skirts, and the little hat perched on her head and tied under her chin. Me, I was wondering how anyone could move in such a get-up, let alone try walking on ice.

Her father's jaw tightened. 'Beloved, after everything that has befallen us, would I risk your safety? Well, *would* I?'

The girl's face paled in a way that got me wondering what *had* befallen them – a tragedy, by the looks of it – though my chief concern was whether her father was right that the ice was safe. He was standing on it now, offering his hand to help her down the bank.

Reluctantly, she hitched her skirts and joined him. Funny though, she didn't take his hand.

The ice held, but proved near impossible to walk on. Just a few steps in and the man's feet went from under him. He landed with a thump on his backside. I had to choke down a laugh, because it *was* funny, especially seeing his beautiful cloak getting tangled in his feet.

'Stand still! Take my arm! Not like that!' he hissed crossly to his daughter.

Eventually, she got the man back on his feet, and I lost them to the crowds. And good riddance too. If that's what fathers were like then I was glad I'd been raised only by Mother.

*

Now that walking on the ice had lost its appeal, I was thankful to find the hiring fair in its usual place on my side of the river. There were farm hands and kitchen maids, grooms and carpenters, all recognisable by the tools of their work, which they'd laid out at their feet. I felt a bit daunted, then. I'd nothing to display but Mother's parcel, which I didn't suppose would help. But I remembered what she'd said about boys getting better-paid work, and stood squarely, chin up, ready to put on a gruff voice when someone spoke to me.

Business was brisk. It was obvious who was doing the hiring. You simply looked for the smartest coats and the loudest voices. Farmers, estate owners, housekeepers were barking out questions at whoever had caught their eye – 'How old are you? What can you do? How much do you eat?' – and checking hair, teeth, if a person had had the smallpox.

I waited. No one spoke to me. No red-jowled farmer shouted in my face. No housekeeper knocked the cap off my head to inspect my short hair.

Once the strongest, cleanest workers were hired, it was only the stragglers left behind – the old, the scrawny, the ones too sick to stand up – and me.

'How old are you, child?' a farmer demanded. 'Can you kill a pig?'

'He looks rough enough,' smirked another. Then he noticed Mother's parcel, which I was hugging to my chest. 'What've you got in there?'

Before I could answer, he'd hooked his cane around the package. A quick flick sent it flying up into the air. It landed some way off in the gutter.

'Hey!' I cried. 'That's mine!'

As I lunged for the parcel, someone's foot got there

first. And I found myself eyeballing yet another pair of leather boots, only these ones were smaller and scruffier than the soldier's.

'Not so fast,' said their owner, pulling me upright. 'You, boy – you got a name?'

It took a second to find my tongue. The voice addressing me wasn't a Somerset one. It was rich and warm: sunshine and canary wine. And this person, dressed in breeches, long boots and a black wool coat, was in fact a young woman. She had the brownest skin and brightest eyes I'd ever seen.

'Ummm ... errr ... Fortune Sharpe,' I said, swiftly adding, 'It can be a boy's name too.' I'd no idea if this was actually true.

The woman looked narrowly at me. 'Hmmm. Then no wonder this belongs to you.' The parcel, in all its grisly glory, now lay open in the flat of her hand.

I took a very deep breath. 'And who are you, Mistress ... ?'

'Maira. Just Maira.'

It wasn't a Somerset name, either. Other people were studying her now – her different clothes, her skin, her tall, upright frame. She wasn't one of them, one of us. She stood out from the locals like gold amongst pewter.

'Do you know what this is?' she asked, meaning the dead skin inside the parcel.

'A bit of lung, maybe? My mother gave it to me on the way here. She said it was mine.'

'Which explains why you were named Fortune.'

I almost laughed out loud. I was cold, hungry and rather bewildered: I certainly didn't feel especially fortunate.

Yet this Maira woman wasn't like the bawling farmers or the housekeepers with their eagle eyes. Her waist-length hair and men's clothes made her look magnificent. I didn't know if I was scared or in total awe.

'Are you having the boy or not?' the farmer wanting a pig-killer asked.

I had to think fast.

'Don't let the parcel put you off. I'll get rid of it, if you'll hire me,' I begged Maira.

She stared at me. 'You must NEVER do that!'

'But surely it's only dead skin, so—'

'Listen to me,' she interrupted, fierce enough to make me flinch. 'Your mother was a sensible woman in keeping it, unlike her child.'

I frowned at her, at the thing in her hand.

'Still want to work for me, then, do you?' she asked, her tone softening a little.

I nodded, though didn't think to ask what I'd be doing. As long as it wasn't pig-killing, I didn't much care.

'Come, then,' she said, beckoning urgently for me to follow. 'We must away.'

Yet before I could take a step, someone gripped my shoulder. 'You, boy, are taken.'

In the tail of my eye, I caught a shimmer of dark blue velvet. I spun round in alarm.

'No, sir, I'm not for hire,' I told the man who had hold of me.

The rest of the crowd melted back until it was just me, the man in the cloak and his daughter, looking less than impressed.

'I'm already taken,' I tried to explain. 'This woman's going to hire me.'

Except when I turned to Maira, she wasn't there. She'd disappeared with my parcel still in her hand.

II

IN WHICH OUR HERO DISCOVERS TWO SECRETS AND HAS HER OWN REVEALED

9

The man eyed me up and down, like I was an animal and he was considering my worth. It made me shrink deep inside my clothes.

'A scrag-end of a boy,' he said, tapping his foot. 'Hmmm . . . You'll do very well. Just the sort of servant I'm after.'

He set off towards his waiting carriage, expecting me to go with him. I stayed where I was. Surely he had to bargain with Maira, who'd as good as already hired me: that was how it worked. Yet neither she nor my parcel was anywhere to be seen. I felt flustered and suddenly angry.

Had I been tricked?

Had Maira wanted to rob me rather than hire me?

What annoyed me most was my own stupidity. I was an idiot. I'd been dazzled by her sunshine voice and gentleman's swagger and now, in her possession, was the one item I had from home.

'That woman, she's got something of mine!' I pleaded to the man's daughter, who was trying to hurry me towards the carriage.

'Well, she appears to have gone now,' the girl answered, as if that put an end to it.

'But she's a thief!'

'I don't care *what* she is,' the girl muttered irritably. 'Though why Father had to hire the scruffiest, oddest-looking creature in the whole fair I'll never know.'

'I didn't ask him to pick me!' I retorted.

The girl seized my arm. 'We're stuck with you now, so come on. We mustn't keep my father waiting.'

I didn't have much choice but to swallow my anger and go with her. Being a servant to this man had to be better than butchering pigs, and that was the choice I faced.

*

I'd never been inside a carriage before. And I only did so now because every inch of outside space held items bought from the market – a bolt of cloth, a basket of chickens, boxes, all of which had already been tied down for the journey ahead. Being Mr Spicer's final market-day purchase, there was no room left for me.

'Must he sit inside?' the girl complained, fanning her nose.

I ignored her, concentrating on the carriage instead. The seats – more rich velvet – were as hard as a stone floor, the walls papered in rose patterns. It was smaller than I'd imagined. Smellier too – a nose-tickling mix of hair oil, dust and soap. Spread out on one of the seats was a piece of sewing, complete with coloured threads.

'That's mine,' the girl said, snatching it up as if she didn't want me to see it.

She needn't have worried: I wasn't interested in needlework. Back home, I was the one who tore holes in things, and it was Abigail or Mother who sewed them up again. But, I remembered fast, I was a boy now, and boys didn't have to explain why they hated sewing.

Yet I still caught myself staring at the cloth in her hand.

'My daughter has a rare talent for crewel work, as you've noticed,' the man commented.

Not normal needlework, then, but something finer and more detailed. From the bit I could see, she'd sewn a scene with people and trees, and a river. It was pretty, I couldn't deny it, but how anyone would have the patience for such work I'd never know.

'It's difficult,' the girl said. 'And private.' With that, she rolled it tightly and hid it up her sleeve.

Once we were settled in our seats, the door closed on the crowds and the cold. The horses strained against their harness, the carriage lurched forward, and we were on our way. The daughter and I were squashed together, her big skirts foaming over my legs. It felt odd to be so close to a girl who wasn't Abigail. She smelled cleaner than my sister, her elbows were sharper, and she scowled like a small angry cat.

She was, I decided, the sort of girl I never wanted to be – perfectly groomed, spoilt, ill-tempered.

Her father, I soon learned, was called Mr Spicer, and she, Susannah. When I told him my name, he studied my face for the first time, and I him in return. He was handsome, I noted, though his expression was changeable: in the short time I'd known him, I'd already seen flashes of temper there, and charm.

'Fortune?' Mr Spicer frowned. 'Isn't that a girl's name?'

'It can be either, sir,' I said quickly.

'Well, I trust your character is befitting of such a virtuous title.'

'I try, sir,' I replied. Being virtuous wasn't one of my strong points, but since I wasn't a boy, either, I didn't suppose another lie would hurt.

Anyway, he seemed convinced, and I sat back in my seat, relieved to have passed this first test. Though I didn't feel so clever when Mr Spicer called to the driver, 'Straight home,' and a blast of longing hit me.

When would I return to Fair Maidens Lane? In weeks? Months?

My chest tightened as I thought of Jem, who'd be awake by now, wondering where I was. The sooner I started earning a wage, the quicker I could go home. But what *would* things be like between us when I got back? Perhaps they'd already changed too much.

*

We travelled in bone-rattling haste. The road was frozen hard, made rougher by the potholes, loose stones and sheets of ice that made the wheels skid. Crushed together inside, we were constantly bumping knees, knocking shoulders.

'Pardon me,' I'd mutter each time I fell against Susannah. And each time, her frown would get a little tighter, and she'd shuffle away from me as far as the tiny space allowed.

Don't think I like it, either, I wanted to say, but held my tongue.

Beyond Bridgwater, we followed the river almost as far as the mudflats on the coast. I was torn between feeling queasy and wanting to gaze out of the window at the view. When the horses slowed to a brisk trot, we turned inland. The carriage creaked as we wound in and out of woodland, across open heath and through small grubby villages not unlike my own.

The rocking of the carriage, and the fact I'd had little sleep the previous night, began to make me drowsy. Yet my brain refused to slow down. I'd picture Mother's face with the sword against her nose. And the parcel she'd given me lying open in Maira's hands. And then back to Mother going home to Jem.

When Susannah announced we were nearly there, I was relieved to sit up and clear my head.

The bright daylight outside turned suddenly dim. Instead of open countryside, we were now travelling through a sheer-sided valley – all grey rock and gorse – and seemed to be passing very close to the edges of it. The carriage was going much faster too.

We were plunged into near-darkness. I gripped the edge of my seat. In truth, I feared the horses had bolted with fright and were about to drive us straight into the hillside. Yet just as suddenly, we burst back out into daylight again. The sun was still shining weakly. Frost lay as thick as snowfall on the grass. Up ahead at the curve of a driveway was a long, low house, with so many windows glinting in the light it almost looked as if it was on fire.

'Berrow Hall,' Susannah said by way of explanation. She looked happier suddenly, like any girl might who was glad to be home. I tried not to remember how that felt.

The carriage swung by the front entrance. As it slowed to walking speed, Susannah flung open the door and leaped out on to the drive.

'For heaven's sake, child, can't you wait a moment longer? Have some decorum!' Mr Spicer cried after her.

I watched through the window, a little bit impressed. For such a frail, pampered creature, she could certainly run. Skirts bunched in her hand, she bounded up the front steps to a woman in an apron and cap, who was holding a baby.

'My daughter has her mother's flighty nature,' Mr Spicer observed.

'Is that Mistress Spicer?' I asked, indicating the woman now handing the baby over to Susannah.

'Mistress Spicer is dead,' he said coldly.

I sat back in the seat, wincing at my mistake. 'Well, that's a bonny baby.'

'She's another daughter, more's the pity,' he replied, in the same cold, flat tone. 'My wife died in childbed. My eldest daughter has taken on the responsibility of looking after ... well ...' He sighed, rubbed his brow. 'I don't wish to be bothered with another child, you see.'

I didn't see. But, wary as I was of putting my foot in it again, I kept quiet. Besides, Mr Spicer was keen to move on.

'Now listen to me, and listen carefully,' he said, businesslike again. 'Your position here will be as a personal servant to my only son, Ellis Spicer. He's sixteen years of age and hasn't quite ... *found* himself yet.'

I nodded, even though I didn't quite catch his meaning. Being a servant to his son was a decent job, all right – far better than butchering pigs or milking cows.

'My son will inherit my wealth,' Mr Spicer went on. 'Therefore, it is our responsibility to ensure he grows into a fine young man.'

'Yes, sir.'

It was the way of things in this world, I knew that, though it didn't always make sense to me, the way boys got chosen over girls. When Jem became the favourite to lead our community in Fair Maidens Lane, he didn't even want the position.

Perhaps Mr Spicer's son was different.

10

The carriage deposited us in a courtyard so spotless you could've eaten supper off the cobbles, and I was ravenous enough to do just that, had anyone offered. In amongst the sweet smell of horses and hay was a saltiness I knew all too well. It made me glad and homesick all at once.

'We *are* on the coast?' I asked. On the drive here I must've lost my bearings, because I had been sure we were still some way inland.

'Right by the sea,' Mr Spicer confirmed. 'We're eight miles north of Bridgwater.'

I realised I was further from home than I'd ever been in my life. Though I didn't get to dwell on it as Mr Spicer hurried me around to the back of the house, through a walled garden, under an archway and up some steps to a low studded door that was clearly the entrance for household servants. As we walked, I wondered what Master Spicer would be like – not ill-tempered like his sister, I hoped, for it was dawning on me that I knew nothing of the ways of daily bathing or keeping clothes fresh, or whatever a rich boy might require. In fact, it troubled me enough to say so.

'Not wishing to speak out of turn, sir,' I said, as Mr Spicer strode ahead. 'But wouldn't a boy like your son be better with a proper trained servant?'

'Aha!' Mr Spicer spun round, his handsome face lit up. 'You've hit upon it! My son is of an age where he needs more male influence.'

I gulped.

'A proper, rough-at-the-edges sort of boy, to help him become more ...' He paused, '... *manly.*'

'Manly,' I repeated in my best deep voice.

So my position here was to teach the young Master Spicer how to become a better *man*? I, who'd been raised by strong women, and who, despite my short hair and flat, skinny body, was a girl. It was a job not to laugh at the craziness of it.

'Well?' Mr Spicer stopped on the threshold. 'Is everything clear?'

As clear as sea fog, I thought, though I nodded yet again, like the good servant I was trying to be.

*

Inside, I was taken to an enormous kitchen. The fireplace was so big Jem and me could've stood in it, and the ceiling went up and up to the heavens like a church roof. All the maids chopping, banging pans, scrubbing vegetables, talking, filled the room with a deafening buzz.

The moment they saw us – or rather Mr Spicer – everything stopped. Like puppets, the maids turned their faces to whichever wall was nearest, and an eerie hush fell. Just one woman, so red-cheeked she looked parboiled, came forward. She was the same person I'd seen earlier handing the baby to Susannah.

'Ah, Mistress Bagwell,' Mr Spicer greeted her.

'Good day to you, sir,' she said, bobbing stiffly. 'The surgeon is already here. He made swift time from Glastonbury.'

'Excellent.' Mr Spicer nodded. 'And remember, my son mustn't have anything for the pain.'

Mistress Bagwell sucked in her cheeks. 'Not afterwards? Nothing at all?'

'Nothing. I forbid it. We mustn't pander to his weaknesses. Fortune has been hired to tend Master Ellis from now on. No doubt he'll toughen the boy up.'

And I was promptly handed over to the woman who seemed to be both housekeeper and nursemaid, rolled into one.

Once Mr Spicer had gone, the whole room seemed to let out a breath.

'Back to it, girls!' Mistress Bagwell clapped her hands, then looked me up and down, and properly too, like those housekeepers at the hiring fair.

She sniffed. 'You haven't seen water for a while, have you, lad?'

'I got wet in the sea yesterday,' I reassured her.

She wrinkled her nose. 'Soap, that's what you need.'

She yelled to a kitchen maid to follow us to the washroom with a pail of warm water, then took me down a passageway, past a stillroom full of jars and bottles and the meat room where whole lambs and sides of pig hung from the ceiling hooks. There was so much to see, my eyes were jumping out of my head. Mistress Bagwell threw open a door on a tiled chamber and told me to strip off.

I didn't move.

The maid put down her bucket. From her apron pocket, she produced a cake of soap. She'd also brought a clean shirt and breeches, which she hung on the back of the door. She wasn't in any hurry to leave, either.

'Go on, lad, get washing,' Mistress Bagwell urged.

There wasn't a chance in hell I could risk getting undressed in front of these two.

67

'You don't need to stay,' I insisted, thinking of what my nakedness would reveal.

The maid snorted. Mistress Bagwell rolled her eyes.

'Would you at least mind not staring, then?' I asked.

That set them off into gales of laughter.

'Oh, bless him, he's a shy one!'

'Must have something to hide, mustn't he, eh?'

Too right I did.

I was on the verge of point-blank refusing to wash when another maid came running in, shrieking about the bread having burnt and could the missus come quick before the whole kitchen went up in smoke.

They went, thank goodness, though I didn't trust them not to come back again. I splashed the water over myself so fast it was more of a dampening than a proper wash. The clothes they'd left me, though too big, were of good cloth and clean. With a bit of tucking in and rolling up sleeves, I managed to look half decent.

'You'll do,' Mistress Bagwell observed, when I appeared back in the kitchen.

My stomach made a yowling sound.

'Any chance of a bite to eat, missus?' I begged.

She shoved me on to a stool at the kitchen table, before pushing a plate of burnt bread and butter in front of me. I ate the lot.

'Anything else?' Mistress Bagwell asked, eyeing my empty plate. 'Roast swan? Pigeon pie? A cup of mead for the young gent?'

I wiped my mouth and shook my head.

'At least you've got a strong stomach. That's something. Let's go and meet Master Ellis, then, shall we?' She said it as if the two things were connected.

11

We were halfway up the stairs when the yelling started.

'Get that hook away from me! I'm warning you!'

It was coming from a bedchamber up on the first floor and made me freeze, mid-step.

'Who the devil is *that*?' I asked.

'Master Ellis, making a fuss,' Mistress Bagwell replied, and kept climbing the stairs as if it was all perfectly normal and people hollered their lungs out here every day.

So this was the boy I had to toughen up, though by my reckoning he sounded fierce enough already. I was beginning to wonder what sort of house I'd come into.

At the door to Master Ellis's bedchamber, Mistress Bagwell turned to me.

'He's not a bad boy,' she said, softening. 'His father sometimes forgets he's still feeling the loss of his mother.'

The door swung open on to a room that smelled of blood. Glimpsing round Mistress Bagwell's shoulder, I couldn't see a boy, never mind a bleeding one. I took in the high bed with its tapestried hangings, the leaping fire, the wood of the tables, walls, floor, all polished to perfection.

And then, the tooth-barber.

He was by the window. Despite being rather short, he managed to block out a good deal of light.

'Just a back tooth removed today,' he said to Mistress Bagwell. He had a strong local accent, soft and meadowy, which was at odds with the blood on his bare forearms. 'More teeth-cleaning, less sugar-eating, that's what this young man needs.'

Mistress Bagwell sucked in her cheeks like she didn't agree, but replied, 'Very good, Dr Blood.'

The name was fittingly grim.

From the bed, someone groaned, then spat. There was the sound of something solid hitting a pan. Master Ellis, I saw now, was tucked away in the far corner of the mattress, like an animal that was hurting. I didn't blame him, either – Dr Blood had a brutal look about him that wasn't only on account of his trade. He made the hairs at the back of my neck twitch.

'I trust you have hot water and soap ready for me?' Dr Blood asked.

'Indeed.' Mistress Bagwell opened the door, indicating that he should go with her.

And so he did, though as he passed he glared at me as if every tooth in my head needed pulling. Instinctively, I clamped my mouth shut.

Once they'd gone, and I was alone with Master Ellis, I moved nearer the bed.

Be polite, I told myself, don't pick your nose, don't chew the ends of your fingers where the skin sometimes flakes, and for goodness' sake don't stare.

'Are you well, master?' I asked, which was stupid to say but the first thing that came into my head.

Shuffling into a sitting position, he regarded me with huge grey eyes that even then glinted with mischief. I stared back – I couldn't help it. He looked so much like Susannah, only a couple of years older, with brown hair that didn't curl, and a face more given to smiling.

'Who are you?' Master Ellis spoke like his mouth was full of padding.

'I'm Fortune.'

'Intriguing name for a boy, though you don't appear very fortunate,' he commented.

Nor do you, I thought. His cheeks were whiter than

clean laundry. A couple of thumb-sized bruises were coming up nicely on his jaw where the tooth-barber had gripped it.

'Your father has hired me to be your servant,' I said, just so he knew I wasn't anything to do with Dr Blood. 'He says I'm to help you become more of a man.'

A look flashed over Master Ellis's face – part indignant, part amused.

'More of a *man*, eh?' he said, considering it. 'Did my father speak those very words?'

'Ummm ... well, yes ... in a way ... ' But the more I tried to explain the more knotted my tongue became.

Anyway, Master Ellis was already laughing.

'Oh, that's quite the finest thing I've ever heard!' he cried.

'Is it?' I was confused.

'Oh yes! Thank you, Fortune. I haven't laughed that much in months!'

Maybe it was nerves or tiredness or the fact I rather liked him, but Master Ellis's laughter made me start to giggle. So when the bedchamber door opened and Susannah flew in, she found the pair of us cackling like old hens.

'Oh!' She stopped mid-stride. The baby was with her, bound in cloth and tied to her chest like working women did with theirs. 'I see you've met our new servant, Ellis.'

Ellis wiped his eyes. 'Dear sister! Can you believe it? Fortune here is Father's latest attempt to turn me into the perfect son. No offence meant, Fortune,' he added to me.

'None taken, master,' I said, though now the laughter had stopped I was confused all over again. I felt shifty too: Susannah watched me with the sort of cleverness that saw straight through my disguise. I was glad when her attention switched to Master Ellis's tooth.

'Oh, Ellis, did it hurt?' she asked, climbing up beside him on the bed. From deep inside the folds of cloth, the baby gurgled.

'Agony. I despise that wretched man,' Ellis replied, then said to the baby, 'Greetings, Busy Bea! You've come to entertain me too, have you?'

The baby, hearing his voice, squirmed enthusiastically. They looked a close, affectionate family all together like that, and it made me miss my own. Even Susannah was smiling, which made her whole face change. At least it did until she realised I was still here, standing awkwardly by the bed.

'Have you no work to do?' she asked sharply.

'I'm to tend Master Ellis,' I said.

'His bedclothes need replacing. See to it, will you?'

But as I came closer she changed her mind.

'Oh, I'll do it. Here, take Bea.' She was already unwrapping the baby and holding the wriggling creature towards me.

'No, miss, I'll do the bedclothes,' I replied quickly.

From the smirk on Master Ellis's face I guessed I'd spoken out of turn. But I was wary of babies, not like Abigail, who crooned and clucked every time she saw one at market. In truth, I found them slightly terrifying.

With Master Ellis moved to a nearby chair, I set to work on the bedclothes. There was clean linen in a chest at the foot of the bed – bedsheets, pillow slips, mattress covers, top sheets. I'd no idea rich people slept under so many layers of cloth, or how to arrange them. By the time I'd finished the bed was no neater, but at least it was clean.

Master Ellis crawled between the sheets groaning in discomfort.

'Fetch me something for the pain,' he pleaded.

'A glass of port wine?' Susannah suggested.

'My mother swears by yarrow root for toothache,' I said, scooping up the soiled linen. 'Or willow bark, and a touch of vinegar for infection. Tastes vile but it works wonders.'

Susannah fired a look at Master Ellis. He tried to say something, but his mouth had filled with blood, and he needed to spit it out. I pushed the pan in front of him with my foot.

'Fetch the port wine from the kitchen,' Susannah instructed me.

'But, miss,' I suddenly remembered. 'Your father said no pain relief—'

She looked at me. 'Fortune, you don't seem the type to follow every single rule. Am I right?'

Under that knowing gaze of hers, I felt nervous again.

'I'll see what I can do,' I mumbled, and hurried out of the room.

With the door closed behind me, I paused just long enough to take a deep, deep breath. Inside the room, the hum of voices started up. I didn't mean to listen but they were talking about me.

'You know Fortune is usually a girl's name, don't you?' This was Susannah.

I froze.

Ellis mumbled something I didn't catch.

'Really, brother, I don't know what Father was thinking of, hiring such an imbecile to tend you,' Susannah went on. 'We're a wealthy, landowning family, not an alms house for the poor.'

I glowered at the door.

'I like Fortune,' Ellis answered. 'He's got spirit. Though I can't imagine what Father's hoping to achieve with him.'

'Well, I believe he's hiding something,' Susannah said.

'And we're not, I suppose?' Master Ellis replied.

There was a shuffling. A sound of floorboards creaking.

'Though if Father heard him recommending herbs like that, he'd put him out of the house in a moment.' This was Master Ellis again.

'Really!' Susannah's temper flared. 'What happened to our mother had nothing to do with herbs!'

'No, but Father's convinced it did.'

'Then he's wrong,' she snapped.

The baby started crying. A proper roar it was too, like the world had suddenly ended. Remembering my errand, I hurried away.

*

Down in the kitchens, I found Mistress Bagwell swilling out a bucket of bloody water. The tooth-barber, thankfully, appeared to have gone.

'Messy work, tooth-pulling,' she sighed, taking the

sheets from me and filling more buckets. 'Especially when *he's* doing it.' Which I took to mean she didn't think much of Dr Blood, either. I'd already made a note to keep out of his way.

'What do you make of our young master, then?' Mistress Bagwell asked. Like my sister, she had a nose for gossip, which might be useful, especially in a house like this, where I knew nothing yet and was feeling it keenly.

'He's probably not at his best just now,' I ventured.

'True enough,' she agreed. 'What with his poor mother dying and leaving a baby, and he was already so angry at his father.'

'What about?' I asked, keen to hear more.

We were back in the kitchen now. Mistress Bagwell, having guessed I'd been sent down for wine, took a bottle from a high-up cupboard and poured some into a tiny glass without spilling a drop.

'All this, that's what he's angry about.' Mistress Bagwell gestured to the pewter plates, the meat, the locked cupboard where sugar was kept. Everything breathed luxury and wealth. 'One day Master Ellis will inherit everything – the house, the staff, his father's business – and he doesn't want any part of it. It's bought with merchant's money, you see, got from trading sugar.'

'Mr Spicer trades *sugar*?' She might as well have said gold. Everyone wanted sugar these days, but only the very wealthiest could afford it, which was probably why rich people like Master Ellis had rotten teeth.

'Does that tooth-barber come here often, then?' I asked, hoping he didn't.

She pulled a face. 'Often enough. Dr Blood's an acquaintance of Mr Spicer's mainly, an investor, like, so he's mostly here on sugar business. Master Ellis despises him.'

'So I gathered.'

'To be fair, he did need that tooth pulled today,' she confided. 'It's the business side of things he's most unhappy about. Mr Spicer and Dr Blood have ambitions, you see, to expand trading.'

With a glance over her shoulder, she dropped her voice, so I guessed we were getting to the nub of the matter.

'They're trying to get the backing of King James himself. But father and son don't agree on the king's views, either.'

'Because of the new Bible?' I asked. There'd been plenty of cross words over King James's new version of God's book, even in Fair Maidens Lane.

'Not just that. Mr Spicer thinks wise women are evil. After what happened with his wife.'

'When she had the baby, you mean? When she died?' I asked, wary of where this was heading.

Mistress Bagwell blinked very slowly. 'He got a midwife in to tend her, though it was a difficult birth and a few plants were never going to save her. When she died, he was a broken man. He swears that the herbs poisoned his wife. Claims the midwife was practising witchcraft.'

I gulped, my throat suddenly tight. 'Witchcraft, you say?'

'That's right. He thinks women are a treacherous lot and not to be trusted, any of us. Think yourself lucky you're not a girl.'

12

The next morning, I was under strict instructions to get Master Ellis out of bed for some fresh air.

'Vigorous exercise is the key to building up his strength and creating a healthy temperament,' Mr Spicer informed me. 'My son, you may have already observed, is in dire need of both.'

I'd observed no such thing but didn't argue. I wanted to keep my job, because work meant money. And money meant going home as soon as possible. Though to my mind, Master Ellis had seemed as cheery a soul as anyone could be who'd recently lost their mother and a sizeable back tooth.

On arriving at Master Ellis's bedchamber I found him already up, dressed and in surprisingly good fettle.

'Ah, Fortune! Glad to see you!' he beamed.

I couldn't take my eyes off his outfit. 'You look . . .' I fumbled for the right word, '. . . recovered, master.'

He was wearing a yellow brocade doublet over

scarlet hose, topped off with a sky-blue cap in which waved a ridiculously large feather. I'd never seen so many colours all together, all at once, not even in a church window.

Beneath the smiles and brightness, Master Ellis still looked pale. Yet he was buzzing with energy, rushing about the room, gathering things and humming under his breath. Being used to the sight of farm workers' forearms, I recognised good muscles when I saw them. And Master Ellis might be small, but his shoulders, thighs, calves, were packed with strength, which made Mr Spicer's comments seem way off the mark.

'I'm sorry for asking again, master,' I said, for the matter was perplexing me. 'But this *manly* business your father speaks of. What do you suppose he has in mind?'

Master Ellis laughed drily, gesturing at his outfit. 'Not *this*, that's for certain.'

'But he wants you to be strong and healthy, and to me, you already seem both,' I pointed out.

He folded his arms, looked at me, head on one side like a curious dog.

'You're very direct,' he said. 'And I like you for it.'

'Your father wants to change you though, doesn't he?' I pressed. 'Only it seems to me there's lots of ways of being a man. Take my brother – he's all legs and arms, like a great bony bird, but he's honest and good—'

Master Ellis stopped me with his hand.

'I want to show you something. Carry that, will you?' He pointed to a basket, brimful of what appeared to be ropes and cushions. 'We're going down to the beach.'

This pleased me no end.

'Oh, I do so love the sea! Our shoreline back home is my favourite place in the world!' I gushed. Then, remembering to add, 'Very good, master,' I took hold of the basket. It was far heavier than it looked, and chimed like a clock when I tried to hoist it off the ground. Really, it needed two people to carry it, but Master Ellis was already out of the door.

Susannah joined us at the head of the stairs. The baby was with her again, arching its back and shrieking to be put down. Susannah looked tired.

'You're taking Fortune along?' she asked, surprised. 'Are you sure?'

'Quite sure. I believe my new servant understands me very well,' Master Ellis replied, smiling at me.

I smiled back, not sure I *did* understand, not totally. Yet what I did see was how bright he was, how full of life, and that his father was trying to snuff him out like a guttering candle.

'We'd better come with you,' Susannah said, turning to the baby. 'Hadn't we, Bea?'

Which I took to mean she didn't yet trust me.

*

I had it in my mind that the beach lay on the far side of the woods. But instead of heading for the garden, Master Ellis stopped at the bottom of the stairs. The baby was no longer crying, thankfully. It was as if she sensed where we were going.

'In here, quick!' Master Ellis said, and pulled me through a doorway. Susannah followed as we went down more stairs into a cellar. On the bottom step Master Ellis took another lantern from its hook, lighting it with flint and tinder from his pocket. He beckoned us to the far corner of the cellar, where between us we moved aside a table. Underneath it, set in the floor, was a trapdoor. I felt a stir of excitement.

'Take this,' Master Ellis said, meaning one of the door's rope handles. The other he gave to Susannah, who wrapped it round her wrist.

Putting down the basket, I grasped the rope. Together, on the count of three, we heaved the door, which was as heavy as a slab of stone. As the trapdoor creaked open, I caught a waft of salt and seaweed, a smell as familiar to me as home. Bea seemed to know the smell too, and squealed in delight.

'Stay close behind us,' Susannah instructed. 'And stop grinning like an idiot, Fortune. You'll need to watch where you put your feet.'

Master Ellis went first, then Susannah with the baby. We climbed down one ladder, then another longer one. It was tricky-going. The wooden rungs were slippery and I had to hold on for dear life with one hand, the basket in the other, in danger of dropping everything. Susannah's head was just below my feet, and beyond that Master Ellis's lantern, making little impression on the darkness. It got blacker and damper the deeper we went, until finally the lantern stopped moving. We'd reached the bottom.

We were in a long narrow cave with walls that were solid black rock and so wet with running water they glinted. About two hundred yards up ahead was a keyhole of brightness. I could even now hear the shush of the sea.

'One small thing.' Master Ellis shone the lantern at my face, making me blink. 'You're not to mention we've been here. Father won't approve.'

'If anyone asks, we've been to the woods,' Susannah added.

I wanted to ask why, but felt her eyes on me, daring me to break the fragile trust her brother seemed to be offering.

'Very good,' I answered, and meant it. The truth was, the more I heard of Mr Spicer, the more I warmed to his son. Anyone who loved the beach was decent in my book.

As we burst out into daylight, I breathed in great lungfuls of salty air. The effect was immediate: my head cleared, my shoulders relaxed. The benefits of fresh air were one thing Mr Spicer and I could agree on.

And fresh it was – a bitter cold northerly breeze that quickly numbed my face. The heavy sky made everything look grey: the beach, the grass in the dunes, the sea. Our little cove back home shared this same stretch of coastline, yet the view felt strikingly different. Unlike ours the beach was long and flat, and with the sky up above and the ocean out in front it felt as if we'd all the space in the world.

Beside me, Master Ellis started stretching his arms above his head.

'Just look at that sea,' I murmured as much to myself as to him.

The tide was starting to come in, the waves the gentle, lacy-edged kind that made a lapping sound when they touched the beach.

'Are you going to begin, Ellis?' Susannah called. She'd spread out her skirts to sit at the bottom of the sand dunes. Bea, now free of her wrappings, was on her knee, twisting her hands through Susannah's hair.

With a quick glance back at the house, Master Ellis gestured for me to put down the basket, which I did gladly.

'This is a decent spot, do you see?' he said.

From here all that was visible of the house was its garden wall that ran along the top of the beach like a castle's ramparts. The spot Ellis had chosen was almost directly beneath, so anyone at Berrow Hall looking out of a window would only see beyond us.

Master Ellis flung his hat down on the sand. He started unbuttoning his doublet, excited and maybe nervous in equal measure.

'I'm afraid I have something else to ask of you,' he said.

'What is it?' I wasn't sure where to look, what with him shedding his clothes, so kept my eyes on the sea.

'First, I'd rather you addressed me by my name.'

'I already do, Master Ellis.'

'Ellis, please. My second request involves you keeping another secret, and I think you'll find that easier to do if we're friends.'

'But I'm your *servant*,' I said, rather surprised.

'Indeed, and I suspect you're one of the most honest people in this household.'

I glanced nervously at Susannah, who probably wouldn't agree. I wasn't sure I would, either, standing here in my boy's clothes.

'Yes, master – I mean, Ellis,' I stuttered.

'Good. I find the qualities of friend and servant often overlap.'

I wasn't an expert in either, so bit my lip.

Ellis, meanwhile, was rummaging deep in the basket, cushions, rope, jugglers' balls all spilling out on to the sand. When he found what he was looking for, he held it up for me to see. It was silky, brightly coloured. The sort of costume an acrobat would wear.

'We come here as often as possible so I can practise,' he explained. 'One day, when I'm good enough, I'm going to be a performer in a theatre troupe, or an entertainer, a player. That, my friend, is my lifelong dream.'

'And he's brilliant,' Susannah chipped in. 'Now you've shared your secret, Ellis, you might as well show Fortune a few tricks.'

In a blink, Master Ellis had swapped his doublet for the acrobat's vest. Gesturing for me to stand back, he stood, feet apart, then slowly widened his legs until he dropped to the ground. It looked painful, seeing them split apart like that.

Ellis laughed at me. 'Look at your face!'

But I'd never seen anyone do such a thing before. Next, he was up on his hands, curling his legs right over his head so his toes almost touched his nose. It was incredible. He kept stretching till his feet hit the sand again. Then he crawled like a crab over to Susannah, who was grinning from ear to ear. So was Bea.

A quick backflip. A gracious bow. And Master Ellis stood before me, pink in the face and sparkling.

I was, for once, speechless.

'No one else knows what I do,' Master Ellis warned me. 'My father would disown me if he ever found out.'

'I *bet* he would!' I agreed, for this Ellis – the acrobat, the performer – was worlds away from the son his father was planning a future for. I couldn't help imagining the look on Mr Spicer's face if he ever *did* find out.

'Can you keep the secret?' Master Ellis asked. 'You look as if you might.'

Instantly, I was wary. 'What makes you say that?'

'I'll be honest.' He glanced at his sister. 'Susannah is convinced you're not a proper boy.'

I tried to laugh. 'Bet she says that to all the skinny ones.'

'Just the ones who are girls.'

'Oh.'

I dug at the sand with my foot. There was no point denying what they'd already guessed, though I felt bad for not confessing earlier, and worried they'd have to tell Mr Spicer. So it was a relief when all Ellis did was hold out his hand for me to shake.

'Seems we've both got things to hide,' he said. 'Come, *can* you keep a secret?'

'Can *you*?' I asked in reply.

Susannah, baby on hip, crossed the sand to join us.

'Look at us all,' she said, rather fiercely. 'None of us is exactly *normal* – Ellis, in your bright clothes; you, Fortune, a girl who passes for a boy; and me, well, I don't *feel* like a proper young lady, even though I try.'

She didn't seem like one, either, now I dared to study her properly. Certainly, she wasn't easy to warm to like her brother: if he was sunshine, she was dark, heavy skies. Yet maybe all that temper and scowling was *her* disguise, and beneath her prim face and expensive grey frock was a different Susannah Spicer.

I didn't know. And she certainly gave very little away. But after our conversation on the beach, I watched out for that girl, so that when she did appear, I'd be ready.

13

With each passing day, I began to understand the rhythm of life at Berrow Hall a little more. I worked hard and I didn't ask questions: I didn't need to when some of the answers were so obvious.

Everyone was a little afraid of Mr Spicer. Our sneaking down to the beach each day, our clothes, our whispers, continued apace, though we all knew we'd be in monstrous trouble if we were ever found out. So I was glad of the news, a few weeks after my arrival, that Mr Spicer would be absent from home for a day or two. The grisly Dr Blood was accompanying him.

'Is it sugar business that takes him away?' I asked Mistress Bagwell. We were sitting in the servants' hall, slurping pottage, as we did to break our fast every morning.

'Oh no,' she said, in that dramatic way of hers that warned me I was in for a story. 'They've gone to Ilchester to observe a witch trial. To see how it's done, like.'

I stopped eating.

'Someone here in Somerset is being tried as a witch?'

'Yes, poor woman.' Mistress Bagwell sighed. 'All she did was make better cheese than her rivals, and now they're trying her as an example to others.'

I felt suddenly ill. Mother had always sworn that Old Margaret would come home again – I mean, why wouldn't she, when she'd done nothing wrong? The good women of Fair Maidens Lane were midwives, pig breeders, milkmaids, fisherwomen. There wasn't a single witch amongst them. Never had been. Never would be. All I could hope was that somehow Master Sharpe – my gangly brother – was enough to keep everyone else above suspicion.

*

Had it not been for Susannah and Bea, I would have spent the day fretting over Old Margaret, and imagining worse fates for Abigail and Mother. As it was, Bea wouldn't stop crying. Mistress Bagwell brought lavender water and cold cloths, and when that didn't work, tried sugar mixed with milk. But Bea only twisted her head away and cried more.

All day Susannah walked the baby up and down the stairs, round the house, through the gardens. I hoped the sounds of the sea on the beach below might soothe her, like they'd done to me as a child. But out in the salty air she screamed even harder.

When Susannah grew tired, Master Ellis took over. He sang to Bea, rocked her, kissed her. By nightfall, everyone was exasperated.

'I promised Mama I'd look after her,' Susannah wailed. 'I gave her my word.'

Master Ellis – fretful, teary – took himself off, claiming he had a balancing act to practise. It was then Susannah broke down too.

'There must be something else we could try,' she sobbed.

As I've said, I was rather afeared of babies. Growing up with midwives as neighbours, I was all too aware of the dangers of childbed and how frail new life could be. Many of the graves in our churchyard were the little ones that didn't take the sexton long to dig. At the thought of such a fate happening to Bea, I felt desperate.

'I know what your father thinks of herbs, but we really should try some chamomile,' I said to Susannah.

She was still wary of me, still kept that mistress–servant distance, even though her brother and I were as easy together as old friends. And I could see her weighing it up, thinking over my suggestion, when we'd wasted enough time not treating Bea properly.

'I'm sorry about what happened to your mother, truly,' I pressed her. 'But herbs aren't witchcraft, they're medicine. We've got to at least try – nothing else has worked.'

She wiped her eyes. Nodded as if to gather herself.

'Mistress Bagwell keeps a bunch of dried flowers in the cellar. *Hidden*,' she added, seeing my look, 'behind the apple basket.'

*

The chamomile was easy to find. What was harder was rubbing a tincture of it into Bea's gums. I had more luck than Susannah, which surprised us both, and it wasn't too long before the baby began to look calmer. She even managed a dribbly smile.

'I think she likes you, Fortune,' Susannah observed.

'Ah, I'm no dab hand with babies, miss,' I replied, getting to my feet in case she'd any plans to give me the child.

'Well, they say babies can tell if a person's decent, and I think Bea's decided on you.'

The funny little creature was staring at me, all right, her eyes as dark as nutmegs.

'Thank you, Fortune,' Susannah said quietly. 'For helping with Bea, and for Ellis. He's happier than I've seen him since, well, since Mother died.'

I flapped my hand, in truth a bit embarrassed. 'Oh! Enough, now!'

I went off to the kitchens for bread, cold meat and a jug of small beer because Susannah was looking exhausted. By the time I returned, Bea was fast asleep. Susannah, feet up on a stool, was sewing.

I put down the tray of food, glad as anything. 'Would you look at her now, peaceful at last!'

But Susannah seemed oddly captivated by the square of crewel work that lay in her lap. It struck me as a funny name for something so swirly and pretty.

'Come,' I said gently, 'why not put your sewing aside and have a proper rest? I can turn your bed down and make up the fire—'

'Fortune?' Susannah said, as if she'd not heard me. 'Look at this. What do you see?'

She was holding up the piece of crewel work. I wasn't sure I was the best person to ask, knowing as little as I did about needlework. All I could see was a pale blue curve that looked like a plant stem, and some shapes in red that might've been flowers.

'It's ... umm ... very pretty,' I said. 'Is it a cover for a pillow?' which clearly wasn't the right thing to say.

'It's not *nice*,' Susannah insisted. 'It's peculiar. Can't you see the crying baby?'

I looked again. As she traced the blue curves with her finger, I began to see something that might've been a person's head, or a tree or ... I rubbed my eyes. No, I couldn't see a baby.

'Sorry. It just looks like a pattern to me,' I admitted. 'I mean it's very beautiful and you're proper good at it, but—'

Susannah slumped back in her seat with a groan.

'What is it?' I was worried now. 'What've I said?'

She shook her head. 'It's not you. It's me, over-thinking things again. It's probably a silly coincidence. It's just that sometimes, when I sew ... ' She hesitated, '... the needle has a life of its own. It won't follow the pattern I want to work with.'

'Sounds like my needle every time I try to sew,' I remarked.

'I'm being serious,' she said sharply.

'Sorry.' But I couldn't quite grasp what she was trying to tell me. 'So you mean your needle sews by itself?'

'Yes, it does.' Susannah nodded. 'And then afterwards the picture it's sewn seems to actually come true. It's happened twice now – once at the hiring fair when Father fell on the ice, and now Bea with her teeth.'

It came back to me that day in the carriage, when she'd left her needlework lying on the seat, and snatched it away to hide it up her sleeve. But really, anyone might've slipped over on the frozen river – and I'm sure plenty did. As for babies, well, they cried a lot, didn't they? Neither incident was that unusual, all told.

She must've read my face: putting the crewel work aside, she reached for the bread I'd brought her and started eating.

'You're right,' she said, between mouthfuls. 'Forget what I've told you. It's childish nonsense.'

'Very good, miss,' I agreed.

*

Except I didn't forget, much as I tried to. And the next day, when Mr Spicer returned to Berrow Hall, he brought a darkness with him, which made me feel the weight of Susannah's secret all the more. The mood in the house had changed. A taint seemed to cling to Mr

Spicer – I was certain it came from the witch trial, and in the days that followed, his poor children bore the brunt of it. Ellis was made to watch cock fights and shoot pistols, Susannah to practise needlework until her fingertips bled, and poor Bea was passed between the house staff like an extremely chatty parcel. It wasn't right at all, and I was in a turmoil for wanting to say so. But as I'd not yet been paid my first quarter's wages, it was wiser to keep quiet, though I wasn't certain how much longer I could manage to.

14

Christmastide passed, and before we knew it, Twelfth Night was upon us. Back home we celebrated with wassailing, which involved pouring cider around the apple trees to bless the harvest. The preparations at Berrow Hall were on another scale entirely. Hams were boiled, whole sheep roasted, pastry rolled and cut into shapes. Sweetmeats, marchpane, dates, quails' eggs – everything was arranged on huge blue and white platters. The kitchen was as busy as a bees' hive. Throughout the rest of the house we beat carpets, scrubbed flagstones, decorated mantelpieces and beams with holly from the garden. And suddenly I was everyone's servant, not just Ellis's, with a chorus of 'take this', 'carry that' ringing in my ears.

When the evening of the Twelfth Night party came, I was as excited as anyone. In the Great Hall's fireplace, the yule log blazed merrily, bringing with it all the good luck we could wish for this coming year.

Lute music drifted down from the minstrels' gallery. Surveying it all, I could almost believe the master of this beautiful house was a decent man, who didn't bully his children or attend witch trials. He was a man sad for his dead wife, and tonight would mark a new beginning.

Meanwhile, in the adjoining room a group of brightly dressed actors were putting the finishing touches to their costumes: once supper was served there was to be a mummers' play. Ellis couldn't wait. All day he'd been pacing the Great Hall, moving furniture, asking for more candles, then insisting they be taken away again. Everything had to be just right for the performers, though Susannah and I were the only ones who knew why it meant so much to him.

The guests started arriving at sundown. Eager to see who was coming, I stole a moment with Ellis and Bea, who were watching from a window seat at the front of the house. Since I'd been at Berrow Hall the only person to come calling was Dr Blood, who, sure enough, was amongst the first to arrive.

'Might've known he'd be here,' Ellis muttered irritably.

'I suppose your father invited him,' I reminded him.

'But he's not a friend.'

'Business partner, then.'

The driveway was thick with traffic. Horses, carriages, a sedan chair all inched towards the house in a parade of lanterns and extravagant party costumes. Bea was fascinated. Hands pressed against the glass, she insisted on standing unsteadily in her brother's lap. It was all she ever wanted to do these days – stand up, wriggle about, chat away. And if anyone ignored her, she'd squeal a high-pitched 'Eeeeeeeeh!' so usually it was worth letting her have her way, just to save your ears.

'You know my father and Blood are loyal to the king, don't you?' Ellis said, still on the same subject.

I did: Mistress Bagwell had said as much.

'My father is trying to find a shipper to take a special cargo across the Atlantic Ocean.' Ellis's jaw tensed, just like his father's. 'And he's after the king's assistance – his navy, to be precise.'

'What, ships with guns on board?'

Ellis nodded. He didn't often speak about sugar trading, so it must have been bothering him. 'His usual shipper won't work with him – and you can't just hire anyone. They've got to be trustworthy.'

'Because of thieves?'

'Or pirates. Or Spaniards. Or even the shippers and traders themselves.'

It hadn't occurred to me that the seafaring life would be as full of rogues as a Bridgwater back street.

'I won't have any part of that world,' he said firmly, and a bit desperately. 'If Father keeps trying to force my hand I'll run away. I mean it. I'm sick of how he treats me.'

I'd never heard him speak like this before, and I confess I was worried.

'Just don't do anything hasty,' I replied.

I was still mulling over what he'd said when Mistress Bagwell came to find me.

'Quickly now, lad,' she said, bustling me to my feet. 'There's work to do.'

*

Once the guests had all arrived, the feasting began in earnest. Bowls of punch, spiced biscuits, capons, hams, white bread, custards and possets, a vast dish of fruit filled the table, the centrepiece of which was a cone-shaped, brownish lump. Though it didn't look appetising, that lump was a sugar loaf. Mistress Bagwell cut me a sliver when no one was looking, and the taste was like gold dust on my tongue.

It was no big surprise that Mr Spicer was a charming host. As he moved amongst his guests crowing about his daughter's needlework talents and his son's head for business, both Susannah and Ellis played their parts beautifully.

'Isn't there another daughter?' asked a woman wearing huge ruby earrings.

There was, though she was being cared for in the kitchen, and Mistress Bagwell was under strict instructions to keep her there.

When the Twelfth cake was cut open, it was Ellis and Susannah who found the beans hidden inside. The discovery made them King and Queen of Misrule, and was met with whoops and cheers because, for the rest of the night, they were in charge. Not the adults, not the men. Whatever these two children said, we had to do: it was exactly the type of rule-breaking I approved of.

For the first time all evening, Ellis was smiling. Immediately, he ordered that Bea be brought from the kitchen, and she was soon in his arms, her face smeared with cake.

'Ladies, gentlemen, I declare Susannah the King of Misrule!' Ellis cried. 'She'll be a far superior leader to me. I'm very happy to be her queen!'

It was meant in high spirits, and was taken so. People laughed. Glasses were raised. The mood was joyous – deafeningly so. Mr Spicer was easy to spot, being the only person looking decidedly stony-faced.

Susannah, embarrassed by the attention thrust on her, asked for quiet.

'My one request this evening is that you all have fun. Enjoy each other's company, accept each other. Tonight, we don't care for rules.'

A huge cheer went up.

'If you find my misrule isn't to your taste, then I suggest you take yourself off to the garden where it cannot offend you.' Though she didn't look at her father, the message was needle-sharp.

Next, it was the turn of the mummers. Their performance, about a dragon and a knight, was a bit lost on me because I kept having to fill people's glasses. But I could see Ellis at the front of the crowd, Bea on his hip, both totally spellbound. Mr Spicer, meanwhile, was nowhere to be seen.

*

As the night went on, the celebrations grew rowdier. The Great Hall, with its fire blazing, was stiflingly hot and full of sweating, belching bodies. Someone shouted that we should open the windows and doors, and doing so, the party spilled out into the gardens. The cold night air was no longer just for the disapprovers.

In amongst the mayhem, I was still serving drinks. And it was as I walked a loop of the garden, refilling glasses and listening to the waves on the beach below, that I heard two men talking. It was their voices that alerted me – low and tense – and that one of the speakers was Mr Spicer himself.

'It's a sure-fire way to win the king's favour,' he said eagerly. 'You saw what happened at Ilchester, how easily people are stirred up by the merest hint of witchcraft.'

I slowed my step. He was talking about Old Margaret's trial.

'Don't dismiss your daughter's talents, either.' The other voice was Dr Blood's. 'Word has it crewel work is very popular at the royal court. A little gift to His Majesty might not go amiss.'

Mr Spicer went quiet.

'I mean it, man. The shipment should've been here by now, and the other cargo should be on its way to America.' Dr Blood sounded impatient. 'And now everything is delayed. That's what happens when you hire a weak-minded ship's captain.'

'Not weak-minded,' Mr Spicer cut in. 'Far from it. *Too* opinionated, that was the problem.'

'The point is, the cargo is late,' Dr Blood snapped. 'This is *not* how I do business.'

The shift between them was notable. It was Dr Blood who seemed to have the upper hand.

'I believe the witchcraft route is our best chance.' Mr Spicer was circling his argument. 'Find one witch, and hundreds will follow. Somerset is rife with those practising the black arts.'

'So you've said, many times. Though that soldier you hired found no evidence, did he?'

A chill passed over me. Were they talking about the same soldier who'd stopped us on the moors, under orders to seek out *nests of witches*? It seemed a coincidence, but I was more thankful than ever that Mother had got away.

'Then we must have a better plan,' Dr Blood pressed. 'One that will yield impressive results.'

'We could hire a proper witchfinder,' Mr Spicer suggested. 'I hear there's a very effective man operating in Essex, and with his expertise we could make a huge success of this.'

Dr Blood chewed his fingertip. 'That Hopkins fellow? Yes, send word to him. We'll get started with our own men while we wait. That son of yours might be useful too.'

Mr Spicer snorted. '*How?*'

'People seem to like him. They listen to him. He could interview our suspects.'

The shock made me almost drop the wine jug. *Ellis?* He'd not willingly hunt a rabbit, let alone an innocent woman.

'Hmmmm, we could try him. It's about time my son proved his mettle,' Mr Spicer mused. 'I'd hoped hiring a rough sort as a servant might help—'

'That scrap of a lad with the girl's name?' Dr Blood cut in. 'We could put him to use too, taking messages and so forth.'

I must've gasped a bit too loud, for they both looked round and saw me. It took all my courage to step forward with the wine.

'More drink, sirs?' I said, a bit too brightly.

Mr Spicer held out his glass for me to fill: Dr Blood covered his with his hand.

'None for me,' he said. 'I like to keep a clear head when talking business.'

I'd rather he'd been in his cups, frankly, then at least I could've blamed what I'd just heard on the wine.

15

An hour or two past midnight, I finally crawled into bed. Yet try as I might I couldn't sleep. Mr Spicer had been looking for someone to blame since his wife died. Now it was about to happen: a proper witch-hunt throughout Somerset, in which we'd all be given a part to play. Well, I wouldn't do it. And I was certain Ellis wouldn't, either.

When I finally did fall asleep, I was promptly woken by a rush of cold air.

'What the . . . ?' Mistress Bagwell was standing at the foot of my bed in the dim light of early morning, my blankets in her hand. Under the other arm, chattering, was Bea.

I sat up groggily, thinking I'd overslept. 'What hour is it?'

'Never mind that!' She glared at my night shift, at my skinny girl's legs. The look on her face said it all. I felt badly ashamed that she'd discovered my secret like this; I was fond of Mistress Bagwell, and didn't enjoy tricking her. Yet before I'd a chance to explain, she'd thrust Bea into my arms.

'Master Ellis is missing!' Now she was throwing my clothes at me. 'Get dressed! We need to find him!'

'Missing? How?'

'He didn't sleep in his bed last night.' She gave me a stern look. 'Mr Spicer's already furious about the boy's conduct at the party – and you'll catch the blame for that. So if you know what's good for you, you'll find him.'

'Oh mercy!' I leaped out of bed, pulling on clothes.

'I'll alert Susannah. You start searching. Oh, and,' she gave me Bea, 'look after Miss Beatrice, will you?'

'Can't you? You're better at it than I am.' I tried to hand her straight back again, but Mistress Bagwell folded her arms.

'It's about time you did your share of baby-minding,' she said sternly.

'Because I'm a girl?'

'*Because* you're a member of staff in this house!' she cried.

Though she was clearly angry, she did tie a sling for me so I could carry Bea more easily.

'You look after her, mind,' Mistress Bagwell said, kissing Bea's head.

I nodded. I didn't tell her I'd never held a baby in my life.

*

While Mistress Bagwell went to wake Susannah, I hurried downstairs. Bea was surprisingly heavy, her body humid and smelling slightly of cheese. She was also quite drowsy, which helped when it came to climbing down the ladders. By the time I'd reached the beach, she'd gone to sleep. It was a bright, sharp morning. The sky was patched with little clouds, the sea calm and moving lazily over the sand. Shielding my eyes against the sun, I scanned the beach in all directions. If Ellis was still at Berrow Hall, then this was where I'd find him.

If.

What he'd said last night about running away loomed in my head. Would he really take off like that, without a word to anyone? I dearly hoped not, for Susannah's sake at least.

I went right down to the shoreline, scouring the sand, the rocks, the dunes beyond. There was no sign of him anywhere. Yelling his name woke Bea, who copied me, screeching 'Eeeeeewwwwwwwoooo!' painfully close to my left ear. Then she wanted to get down and play in the sand, and when I wouldn't let her, the shouts turned to tears. I jiggled her a little like I'd seen Susannah do, but it didn't really help.

'We've got to find him, grumpy guts,' I told her. 'There'll be big trouble if we don't.'

But once Bea started crying, I knew how hard it was to make her stop. In the end, I turned back for the house, resolved to bribe Mistress Bagwell into taking her again so I could search for Ellis properly. I was almost at the top of the beach when I sighted an odd disturbance in the sand. It was a series of flattened patches, as if someone had rolled over or fallen. And there, caught under a rock, fluttering slightly, was a yellow feather.

Ellis's.

I was startled and relieved, for the marks in the sand were the sort he'd make when practising somersaults or tumbling. How long they'd been there I didn't know. But as it was only a little past daybreak, and Ellis wasn't an early riser, I guessed he'd been here last night. During the party. Before the players, with their songs and acrobatics, had packed up their boxes, loaded their wagon and trundled off into the night.

If Ellis wasn't in the house or on the beach, then he

could have gone with them. Or, said a dark voice in my head, perhaps some horrible accident had befallen him, as happened to my father all those years ago. This coast was unpredictable and wild. A boy out here in the dark might slip, or . . . I shook my head clear. No, Ellis was as fleet-footed as anyone I knew. If he was anywhere, he'd have followed his heart.

I picked up the feather. Somehow, I was going to have to explain what I'd found. What I thought had happened to Ellis. And though I felt low that I might not see him again, that Susannah and Bea might lose their brother, and me my job, I wasn't sad. How could I be when I knew he'd be happier with a travelling theatre troupe than his bully of a father?

Bea had stopped crying. Her little hand reached out to touch the feather.

'What do you think? *Has* Ellis gone with the actors?' I asked her. I truly hoped he had; better that than being dragged into his father's witch-hunt.

At the thump of footsteps, I looked up to see Susannah, still in her nightdress, coming across the beach. She reached us out of breath and agitated.

'Ellis has run away with the players, hasn't he?' she cried.

'It looks that way,' I agreed, showing her the feather.

'He mentioned leaving last night, but I didn't think he'd do it this fast. Did he tell you too?'

'No, he didn't. *This* did.' She shook her fist: in it was another piece of crewel work, covered in dark blue swirls. 'It's happened again, Fortune. I was working on this late last night after the party, and now it's come true.'

I felt suddenly uneasy.

'Show me,' I said.

She smoothed out the piece for me to inspect. All I could see in the needlework were high, arching curves like a huge blue forest, or waves coming up the beach.

'But today's sea is calm as anything, so this can't be right,' I reasoned.

'Here.' She tapped the design where a tiny shape, topped with a flash of yellow, seemed to be fleeing the sea. 'It's Ellis. The needle moved by itself. I couldn't stop it.'

I looked closer. *There*. She was right. It was a boy, running. I stepped back, slightly alarmed. It might be a coincidence – another one – but whatever it was, this thing Susannah's needle did, it was a bit strange, a bit magical, and I dreaded to think what Mr Spicer or Dr Blood would make of it if they ever found out.

'You mustn't show this to anyone,' I said. 'Or tell them what the needle does. Promise me.'

'I'll hide it,' she said, tucking it up her sleeve. 'Though Father's watching my every move.'

'I mean it.' I was firm. 'Your father and Dr Blood want to send your work to the king. I heard them last night, discussing it. It'll be dangerous for you if they do.'

She bit her lip until it whitened.

'I can trust you though, can't I, Fortune?' she asked.

The truth was, I was concerned by how much she'd told me. But I felt so glad that she'd been able to.

'To the grave,' I promised.

Susannah almost smiled, before frowning at me. 'My goodness, I don't believe I've ever seen you holding my little sister before.'

'Mistress Bagwell made me. It's not really helping matters, so I was heading back to the house. She may have news of Ellis by now.'

Susannah stiffened: she'd seen someone on the beach. 'I believe that news is coming our way.'

It was Mr Spicer. From how he strode towards us – arms swinging, jaw set – he was clearly angry.

I'd have to face him sooner or later and explain where I thought his son had gone. Still, I hastily dropped the feather and covered it in sand.

'Go,' I whispered to Susannah. 'You don't need to witness your father tearing me to shreds.'

She shook her head. 'We'll face him together.'

I could hear her quick breathing, and feel my blood pound. Bea, her face squished into my chest, had fallen asleep again.

'Susannah!' Mr Spicer was a good thirty paces away when he started shouting. 'Return to the house!'

She didn't move.

'I mean it!' As he came closer he didn't lower his voice. 'I don't wish to find you here, conversing with your brother's servant!'

She stood her ground.

Mr Spicer stopped in front of us, thunderous. 'Do you defy me? Your own father? Did you not see what a spectacle your brother made of himself last night in that preposterous hat? All because Fortune Sharpe didn't do the job for which he's paid.'

'Ellis looked rather fine, Father.' Susannah tried to calm him. 'And happy. Your guests admired him.'

Mr Spicer was white with fury. '*You*, all three of you, made me look weak. But don't worry, I've plans for you that will wipe those smug looks from your faces.'

'I'm not taking part in any witch-hunt!' I blurted out. 'You can't make me do it. Nor your children!'

'Why, you pox-ridden toad!' He made a grab for me. I felt a rush of air as his arm swung back to wallop me. There was no loud slap. No stinging pain. Susannah stepped between us, blocking the blow.

'Stop it, Father!' she pleaded. 'We should be considering Ellis, not fighting amongst ourselves!'

'Go back to the house, Susannah.' Mr Spicer jabbed a finger at her. 'And find me your very best piece of needlework. That is an order.'

I wasn't listening. I was staring at the shoreline.

Something was wrong with the sea.

III

IN WHICH EVENTS TAKE A DEVASTATING TURN

16

The waves were breaking on the beach, but with none of their usual rhythm, no in and out. They were overlapping each other, spilling sideways, as if the whole ocean was contained in a pan and someone had given it a shake. The sight was strange enough to silence us. Bewildered, we hurried down to the shoreline where the water swirled around our ankles, so eerily like the sea in Susannah's latest crewel work, it made me suddenly afraid. Bea, who'd been woken by our raised voices, started to cry.

'There, there,' Susannah murmured, resting her hand tenderly on Bea's head. I wondered if the soothing was meant for all of us.

Stranger still was how the sea retreated, which it did very suddenly, all at once. I waited for waves to roll in again. Expected it – like one breath following another. But the sea kept shrinking down the beach, going further away from us, until it was just a line of silver on the horizon.

'It must be the spring tide,' I said, for want of an explanation.

Mr Spicer shook his head. 'I've never seen a spring tide retreat in this manner.'

'A storm surge, then?' Susannah suggested.

'Whatever it is, the sea can't just *vanish*,' I said.

Yet it had. I'd seen it happen with my own eyes.

Where the sea had been was now grey, sodden sand. A whole great stretch of it, pitted with little pools. Rocks that had been hidden underwater were dripping in the bright sunshine. And all the time the tide carried on draining away, like an emptying washtub. In all my days of gazing at the sea, I'd never seen it behave so oddly.

Nor had I ever seen Mr Spicer so animated. He was pacing up and down, just like Ellis did when some new idea had seized him and he couldn't keep still.

'This must be an act of God,' he muttered excitedly. 'A punishment for our transgressions. Yes, I do believe that's what this is – a sign from above that our work needs to be done.'

'What are you talking about?' I couldn't hold my tongue. 'It's the sea. It doesn't follow our bidding!'

But Mr Spicer, already lost to his own theory, kicked off his shoes and strode off across the newly wet sand.

Within minutes, he was easily sixty yards out, small as a flea against the empty seabed that stretched in all directions. Perhaps he'd keep walking until he reached Wales on the other side. I hoped he and his poisonous ideas would stay there too.

'There must be a storm coming,' Susannah said firmly. 'We'd best go back to the house and warn Mistress Bagwell.'

'What about Ellis?'

'I feel certain Ellis, wherever he is, is a long way from here by now. Besides, Bea's getting cold.'

The storm idea was certainly a better explanation than Mr Spicer's. The tides had been thrown out by the weather, and we'd do best to return to Berrow Hall, pull the shutters and wait it out.

But I didn't believe it.

How could there be a storm about to arrive when the sky was clear blue and cloudless? There wasn't so much as a breath of wind. Everything was very still. Very hushed. I realised what was missing, then: the gulls.

Normally you'd hear them calling, shrieking. You'd see them too, hovering above a fishing boat or swooping low over the water. You'd catch a flash of white. A yellow beak. A frogspawn eye. Today, there wasn't a single gull in the sky. It was as if they'd kept away on purpose because they knew something wasn't right.

When we turned for the house, I saw them. They were crowding on to a thorn tree. But there wasn't space for them all, so the tree was alive with beaks and flapping wings. Queerer still was the wall of Berrow Hall, on which more gulls sat like soldiers on guard. I'd seen swallows do something similar at the tail end of summer, but this felt eerie and wrong.

I had an overwhelming sense, then, an ice-cold dread, that something very terrible was about to happen.

'What are the birds *doing*?' Susannah asked.

'They're watching something out to sea,' I realised, and we both turned to discover what it was.

The bank of dirty brown-grey cloud on the horizon was coming towards us, billowing like the smoke from damp wood.

It was moving too fast for a sea fog. Instinct made me step further up the beach. Bea was getting heavier, and wrigglier. My back ached from holding her; I wasn't sure if I could for much longer.

'We should go,' I warned.

What we'd assumed was fog or smoke was sea spray. The sunlight caught it, made it shimmer and glisten. It was almost beautiful, until I saw the sea beneath rising up, and how fast everything seemed to be happening. A mountain of deepest blue, getting higher and higher with no sign of breaking. Suddenly there seemed more sea than sky.

'Run!' I screamed.

The sea rushed in at a galloping-horse pace. We didn't stand a chance. One moment I was scrambling up the beach, clutching Bea as best I could, the next I felt as if I'd been hit from behind by a cartload of stone. The force sent me flying, an arrow from a bow. I couldn't scream, couldn't call out, couldn't see where I was going. All I knew was I was moving very fast – so fast I was sure I'd left my guts way behind. Everything was seawater-dark.

When I sensed the surge was easing, I tried to swim. But the sea was in charge, make no mistake. It flung me sideways, pulled me under. Bea was still tied to me, her legs kicking against my ribs. I held on to her with one arm and paddled with the other. I tried to keep both our heads above the surface. And that was a battle enough.

By sheer luck, I spotted Susannah only a few yards away, her nightclothes a white flag in the water.

'Over here!' I yelled. 'Susannah! Over here!'

The roar of the sea was deafening. I felt as if

I had water inside my brain. Each time I shouted, I swallowed mouthfuls. Bea kept kicking. Coughing. I called Susannah's name again, though I'd little hope she'd heard.

'Can you reach me?' I cried.

In desperation, she flung out her arm. I lunged for it. Missed. Tried again, my fingers brushing hers.

'Grab my hand!' I screamed.

For a second, her fingers locked with mine. I felt the pull in my shoulder socket, the heave of the sea. Susannah's terrified face loomed before me. Her blue eyes. Her bluer lips. Then in a surge of foam and mud, she was gone.

17

The more I struggled the harder it got. It was like trying to swim through a wall. I grew quickly exhausted, and was in danger of sinking. Though Bea was still tied to me, she'd gone scarily quiet. I wouldn't let myself think the worst. I didn't even want to look at her – that way, to my mind, she was still alive. All my energy went into staying afloat and keeping both of our heads above the water.

I wasn't on the beach any more. A gatepost rushed by, the mounting steps by the stables, and before I could grasp what was happening, I was over the wall and inside the gardens of Berrow Hall. My first thought was relief: I'd be rescued now by Mistress Bagwell or the other maids. Susannah was probably already in the kitchen, drying her hair by the fire. I tried to grab the top of the wall, the bare branches of the big oak tree. But the sea was too strong: I couldn't hold on for the life of me.

The water snatched up everything in its path. A garden seat swirled past, baskets, the back door torn from its hinges. The ground-floor windows of the house were all smashed in, water streaming inside and then out again, dragging with it chairs, books, pictures, a cup, someone's bonnet. All I could do was get swept along.

At the kitchen window, snagged on the frame, was a maid's brown dress. It looked so real, so like a person, I called out. Yet as the flood carried me closer, I saw, in horror, that it *was* someone. It was Jennet, one of the kitchen girls, face down in the water.

There was no chance for the shock to sink in. Up ahead, another woman lay slumped over a gate. Even before I reached her, I knew it was Mistress Bagwell. Her cap had come off, so her hair – which she always kept neatly hidden – waved in the water like riverweed.

I couldn't get within yards of her body. The sea kept tugging me, spinning me so I was dizzy. I sobbed, gulping in water. Bea was as heavy as stone on my chest, the sling cutting into my neck. I tried at least to float on my back, to keep her from going under, and I was oh so glad when she twitched awake. It helped to have someone to save.

As quickly as I'd come upon it, I left the house

behind. Even in my bewildered state, I knew this wasn't a storm surge, or a high tide. The sea had come too far inland – and was still travelling fast. Out over the fields, I passed trees bent double. A gate on its end. And in amongst it all, animals thrashing and bellowing. I got kicked and barged into, and when a sheep tried to clamber on me, I had to push it away. I was tiring now. Bea was still again, cold and weighty, pressing against what little air was in my chest.

So when I noticed a pig swimming alongside me, I wondered if I'd fallen asleep or worse. I'd never seen a pig in water before. Honest to God, it was a far better swimmer than I was. Jem would've loved it: he had a way with pigs. Said they were cleverer than most people.

Dead animals, carts, gates, trunks, upturned tables floated by. Anything the water picked up lay on top of it like a skin. The whole landscape was covered. I didn't know where the road was, or in which direction the sea lay. I couldn't feel my legs any more. Couldn't stop my head spinning. I kept picturing my family, none of whom could swim. Then I'd remember the steep hill that lay between Fair Maidens Lane and the sea, and I'd tell myself they'd be safe. The doubts would come again and the fear. Round and round like a whirlpool.

It didn't help that bodies were appearing thick and

fast. I'd glimpse an arm, a bonnet, a person caught in a tree so they hung there like a scarecrow. I was terrified I'd see Susannah or Ellis. Yet for every body that wasn't theirs, I felt a tiny beat of hope.

I wasn't even thinking of Mr Spicer when I came upon him. He was caught by his jacket sleeve on a tree branch. The angle of him was all wrong, like a doll that had been flung in temper across a room. His grey eyes were wide open, empty. In a blur, a rush of floodwater, I left him far behind.

*

Another mile, another hour, I'd lost all track of time and distance. The water began to seem gentler, though. I could move my legs against it, float without it sloshing across my face. I'd a moment of feeling almost hopeful. Then the tears came. The shuddering, sickening shock of all I'd seen, all that had happened, and the cold that was wearing me down. And – I couldn't deny it – there was relief mixed in too. With Mr Spicer dead, there'd be no more talk of witch-hunts, at least.

After the tears came exhaustion. With what little strength I had left, I managed to grab on to the bough of a nearby tree. The wood was so rough it tore into my hands. But it floated well and if I heaved enough of myself and Bea out of the water, and lay across it, I could at least rest. Bea didn't stir. I began to drift in and out of sleep.

Half thinking, half dreaming, my head filled with Jem and our disastrous tree-trunk boat. Sometimes I thought myself still crouched inside it, with Jem squatting opposite me, laughing. Then I'd remember all that had happened since, and how I'd never got to say sorry.

18

I must've fallen into a deep, dark sleep, because when I woke up I was lying on grass. My branch and I had come to rest in a steep field. The ground was dry, the grass beneath me warm from the sun, which by now was high in the sky. It was the one thing in this new world I still recognised – that, and the raspy sound of a baby crying. The bundle on my chest moved. Bea!

The little hand reaching out from the sling slapped me square on the chin. Quick as I could, I untied her. Amongst sand, grit, a dead fish, and someone's tasselled slipper caught inside the fabric, was Beatrice Spicer, looking cross and hungry, and more alive than anyone I'd seen these past long hours.

'Bea?' I said her name out loud. 'Little Bea?'

She held up her arms. 'Fuffffaaaaa,' she mumbled, which I decided was definitely 'Fortune'.

I'd never thought myself the type to fall in love with babies. But right then I did, heart first.

*

Beyond our little hillock, the floods stretched in every direction. Here and there, the rooftop of a house poked hopefully above the water, but if the thatch and wood debris was anything to go by, then most of the smaller homes had perished. It was a bleak, nightmarish scene. Yet having Bea to look after spurred me on; I'd need to find food and shelter before nightfall. In the distance, I'd already spotted a church tower perched on an island of green, at least that was how it looked, standing on a steep hill that poked out of the floodwater. It seemed the obvious place to aim for.

'See that?' I pointed it out to Bea. 'When we get there, there'll be hot food and dry clothes, and the biggest fire you ever saw.'

She didn't want to be wrapped up again and cried when I bound her to my chest. But I was tired and weak. I didn't trust myself to carry her in my arms. And to get to that green island, I was going to have to wade or swim through the floodwater that reached all the way to the foot of the hill. By my reckoning the distance was about a mile.

It was a long mile too. Thankfully the water never got above waist height, but by the time I got there, I was exhausted. With the last of my strength, I crawled up the side of the hill. At the top, beyond the church tower, the land fell away to another little hillock, where a few cottages were still standing. I'd never been so glad to see dry walls, dry thatch, smoke rolling out of chimneys. Even better was the smell of baking bread. Bea, grabbing my shirt collar, stuffed it in her mouth. I bet she was hungry too.

'Where in heaven's name have you come from?' a voice boomed from inside the tower.

It took a moment for my brain to catch up. The church wasn't a whole building after all, but the crumbling remains of one. A man scuttled out into the daylight. He was small, round-bellied and dressed in a dusty black coat. He looked familiar – and not in a pleasant way.

'Dr Blood?' I croaked.

'Indeed. Aren't you that servant from Berrow Hall? The one who tends young Master Ellis?' Dr Blood stared at me in amazement.

'I am.' There was no point in denying it. Truth was, I was so maddened by the smell of baking bread I'd have sold my soul to the devil for a bite to eat.

'And,' he waved a hand at Bea, 'this child with you is—'

'Beatrice Spicer, youngest daughter of Mr Spicer,' I said, because as far as I was concerned the days of pretending she didn't exist were over. 'Though Mr Spicer himself has perished in the flood, along with many others. I saw it with my own eyes.'

Dr Blood's face hardened. He muttered something under his breath that might've been a prayer. 'What about his other children?' he demanded. 'The girl with the gift for needlework? Did she survive?'

'I don't know,' I admitted.

He was about to say something else when two women in white caps and rough wool dresses appeared around the side of the church.

'A living child!' The younger one rushed over, and on seeing Bea, cried out, '*Two* living children! We're blessed!' As her arms went around us, I was grateful to her for holding me up.

The woman with her seemed to be her mother since they both had beech-red hair, and the same wide smile.

'We thought the world beyond our little hilltop had ended. Where did you come from?' the woman asked.

'Berrow Hall,' I replied, shivering so hard I could barely speak. 'Mr Spicer's estate by the sea.'

She looked amazed. 'That's got to be fifteen miles from here!'

I could well believe it. If I shut my eyes, I could still feel the power of the water, that sensation of being fired from a bow.

*

The kind woman was called Mistress Cary, her daughter Ellen. They lived in one of the cottages along from the church, which they rented from Dr Blood. He owned most of the land around here, so they told me, and was not a kind master.

'He's our local magistrate these days, and all,' Mistress Cary explained.

Tooth-puller, sugar merchant, landowner, magistrate: there was no end to the man's influence. This latest role was the most worrying of the lot. It gave him the power to hold trials – witch trials – and pass punishments. The thought made me feel a little faint.

Mistress Cary bid me come closer to the fire. 'You need to warm your bones, my sweet.'

Thankfully, she gave us food too. Bea was soon guzzling goat's milk and mashing bread against her face, and I wolfed down a meat pie.

Mistress Cary was sorry that the only dry clothes she

could lend me were girls' ones. In truth, it didn't matter. I didn't need to pretend to be a boy any more. My position at Berrow Hall, and the good coin I'd earned there, had all been swept away by the sea. As for what Dr Blood might think of my sudden change of attire, it barely mattered. I just wanted to feel warm and dry again. Yet when I set about explaining myself to Mistress Cary it came out in a weary muddle, and I started to cry.

'I'm sorry,' I blubbed. 'It's been a very strange day.'

'You're not wrong there,' Mistress Cary agreed. She gave me one of Ellen's woollen gowns, which was as cosy as an old blanket. I couldn't remember the last time I'd worn a dress. The swish of skirts at my ankles was going to take a bit of getting used to.

A heaped plate of bread and honey later, and I began to feel my strength returning. This was despite Mistress Cary's neighbours who had crowded into her house to question me as I ate.

How far did the flood stretch? How many people and livestock had perished?

'I don't know,' I said, over and over.

'All that water came from nowhere,' said a woman with no front teeth. 'No warning. Nothing.'

'Well now, Rose, who could've predicted such a terrible thing?' Mistress Cary remarked.

Susannah, I thought uneasily, that was who.

In my head I could see her crewel work – the swirls of blue, the foaming caps on the waves. This morning she'd insisted it was an omen that Ellis would run away. It was so much more than that now.

Perhaps there was a rational explanation for the flood. Yet when I pictured the sea disappearing and rushing in again like smoke, it wasn't so hard to think magic was to blame. But if Susannah had powers to see into the future, what did that make her?

A witch?

19

The next morning I was woken by a sharp rap on the front door. It was a little after daybreak. Bea and I had spent the night sleeping by the hearth, which was now barely warm.

'All right, all right!' Ellen cried, still tucking her hair under her cap as she opened the door.

Dr Blood came in without being asked; I supposed that was what landlords did.

'I come with solemn news,' he announced, sounding pleased. 'A word with your guest, if I may.'

Moments later, I was facing Dr Blood, the knot in my stomach telling me this news he brought was of Susannah. He'd already asked Ellen to leave the room. I could hear her listening from the top of the stairs, and was glad she was nearby. Bea, who'd insisted on standing, clung to my skirts.

'Thanks to the floodwaters receding overnight on the land beyond the village, a discovery has been made – of ten people, drowned.' He rubbed hands together. The dry, papery sound set my teeth on edge. 'There's a young girl amongst them who may be Susannah Spicer.'

'Have you seen her yourself?' I asked, willing it not to be true.

'No,' he admitted. 'I'm sending you.'

'Oh no, not me,' I begged. I'd seen enough dead bodies to last a lifetime.

'It's not a plea,' he replied. 'It's an order. If the dead girl is Miss Spicer, you'll search her for any needlework she might have about her. It's not fitting for a person of my standing to be seen handling a corpse. You, on the other hand—'

I looked at him sharply. So he was still trying to win favour from the king, even if it meant robbing a dead girl. He was as ruthless as a fox amongst hens.

'I'm not doing it,' I told him straight.

He studied me, taking in Ellen's too-big dress. 'It seems you're not a boy, after all.'

'I've always been a girl. You simply didn't realise.'

He laughed unpleasantly. 'Oh, there's plenty I realise, believe me, especially in people who are a little unusual.'

'I don't work for you, Dr Blood.' I was flustering a little. 'You can't order me to do anything.'

Quick as a finger snap, he grabbed Bea off the floor.

'What—?'

I tried to take her from him but he twisted away so she was out of reach. He was holding her so awkwardly my heart was in my mouth.

'Fuuuffffaaaa!' Bea cried.

'Give her back at once,' I spat.

'Fetch me the needlework, my dear, and you can have the baby,' Dr Blood said.

'And if I don't?'

He held Bea at arm's length, inspecting her like an object, and one that was kicking and turning rapidly red in the face. 'Another drowned corpse shouldn't raise many questions.'

I rushed at him, making a grab for Bea. Whip quick, he twisted away, again, at the same time landing a blow on the side of my head. Everything went blurry. A foot in my ribs sent me sprawling on the floor.

'Fortune!' Ellen cried from her spot on the stairs.

'Just do as he says, child!' warned Mistress Cary, who'd joined her. 'Don't make trouble for yourself, or for us!'

They couldn't help me, I realised, not unless they wanted to risk losing their home.

Bea was crying, holding out her arms and begging

me to take her. I got up slowly, holding my hurting side. Dr Blood opened the outside door.

'Bring anything you find straight to my house in Glastonbury,' he instructed. 'We'll wait for you there.'

He had me cornered. I didn't have much choice but to do as he asked.

*

Since all the other routes from the village were underwater, the road to the common was easy to spot. A track, not quite wide enough for a horse and cart, ran steadily away from the cottages. Despite the early hour, it was already busy with dogs, children, women in bonnets, men in black hats. News of the ten corpses had obviously travelled fast.

Trudging uphill, I grew more distressed. I should've held on tighter to Bea. I should've fought harder. I dreaded seeing Susannah's dead body, and having to search her for the crewel work. All I could do was hope it'd been lost in the flood, because I knew all too well which piece she'd hidden up her sleeve – I'd watched her doing it. Even if she was dead, that piece would still cause trouble. It would fuel the arguments that witchcraft was to blame, and if they couldn't pin the guilt on a dead Susannah, they'd find some other scapegoat.

Up ahead a woman in dark clothes waved for us to stop. She was standing on what seemed to be the brow of a hill, where sheep grazed on, oblivious. I was starting to wonder how the flood could've risen so high and dropped again so fast, when behind her I saw how sharply the ground fell away. About twenty feet down, and glinting in the sunshine, floodwater lay in every direction.

'Only next of kin should come any further.' The woman barred the way with her arm.

Around me discussions started up in earnest about who should go from each family. I held back, not wanting to be the first. All the drowned bodies, cows, pigs, horses, I'd seen yesterday flashed in my head. I couldn't imagine Susannah looking like that, and felt sick all over again.

'You, girl, are you coming or going?' The old woman's voice made me snap to attention.

But she wasn't talking to me. Another girl had appeared, staggering towards us. She was wearing a nightgown – at least, it might've been one once. The garment was shredded at the hem and splattered with mud and goodness knew what. She had a ghostly, staring look to her, even though she was shaking her head at the old woman and saying no, her brother and father weren't amongst the dead.

It didn't occur to me who the girl was until she was almost level with me.

'It's you!' I yelped, throwing my arms round her.

Susannah froze. Then, realising who I was despite my skirts, she hugged me back and burst into tears.

'Oh, Fortune!' Susannah sobbed. 'I was so sure everyone had died.'

Taking her hand, I led her a little way from the crowds. She was shivering, so I put my jacket over her shoulders and gently pushed the hair from her face. I wanted to see her properly, to know it really was her.

'I tried to hold on to you, truly I did,' I said, tears coming.

'I know.' She squeezed my hand. 'But the sea was too strong. I was lucky enough in the end, though.'

'Did someone rescue you? Was it Ellis?'

'No, not him,' she said sadly. 'I clung on to a door and floated with it for I don't know how long. I saw terrible things, Fortune. Things I'll never forget.'

'Me too.'

We stood for a moment, letting everything sink in.

'I have some news,' I said, when she looked a little stronger. 'Grave news. Do you wish to hear?'

'Tell me. I must bear it.'

'Your father, I'm sorry to say, has drowned,' I said. 'And Mistress Bagwell, and Jennet the kitchen maid – I saw them all. I've no word about Ellis, though.'

She squeezed her eyes shut for a moment. Nodded.

'But please, be happy, because Bea *is* alive,' I told her. 'She's in Glastonbury.'

'Oh! Thank goodness!' Susannah's hands flew to her face.

'Dr Blood has her, presently.'

'*The* Dr Blood?' She looked surprised. 'That's very decent of him.'

'There's nothing decent about that man,' I replied. A glance over my shoulder and I dropped my voice. 'Listen, have you still got that piece of crewel work?'

'I have.' She touched her sleeve warily. 'I should burn it, shouldn't I? I don't deserve even to be here after what I've done.'

'This flood hasn't happened because of you,' I told her firmly. 'Whatever you think, whatever anyone says, you're not a—'

'Witch?'

'Shhh!' I hissed in alarm. 'Don't say that word!'

Yet for the swiftest moment, she *did* look unusual – eyes as sharp as daggers in a pale pinched face. Not a witch, exactly, but someone mysterious, who I still didn't feel I knew very well.

'Dr Blood's got it into his head that your crewel work will win him the king's favour. He's desperate to get his hands on it.' I hesitated. 'The problem is, he's holding Bea as a sort of hostage.'

'A *hostage*? Well, he can have my dratted sewing. I never want to see it again.' She started to pull the crewel work from her sleeve.

'No!' I insisted. 'We can't give it to him.'

'*What?*'

'We need to grab Bea – somehow – and get away from here as fast as we can.'

Susannah drew in her chin.

'I refuse to run anywhere,' she said. 'If Dr Blood has Bea, as you say, then I'll simply go and fetch her back.'

I thought of how he'd kicked me to the ground: my rib was still sore from it. 'Susannah, the man holding your sister, who wants your crewel work, is a witch-hunter *and* the local magistrate. He'll stop at nothing to get what he wants.'

She frowned. 'No, he's merely an odious little tooth-puller who happens to be Father's business partner.'

'Exactly.' I took a deep breath. 'He and your father were in it together. I overheard them talking at the Twelfth Night feast, about needing the king's support to get a sugar cargo across the sea, and a witch-hunt is how they plan to do it. Your father had other motives too, as you know.'

Very slowly, she seemed to understand.

'Is this about Mother dying, and the midwife's herbs? Does Father – *did* Father,' she corrected herself, 'want revenge?'

'He did. And now there's all this flooding. Like your father did when he lost your mother, people are looking for someone to blame.'

She grew paler.

'You need to trust me,' I pleaded. 'We'll get Bea and go to Fair Maidens Lane, where my family are. We'll be safe there. My brother will protect us. And we'll try to find Ellis too.'

'You're giving a lot of orders, Fortune,' she remarked.

True, it wasn't the normal way of things for a servant to make the decisions. But then, I'd never seen a gentleman's daughter in a public place wearing only her filthy nightwear, either. The fact was Berrow Hall had gone, and with it the life we'd had there. This new, devastated world of ours was a very different place. Who we'd once been didn't matter so much any more. First and foremost, we had to be survivors, and that meant getting away from here as fast as we could.

20

Dr Blood's house suited him. The long, low red-tiled building had a look of a lair about it, and its twisted chimneys and tiny latticed windows made the inside seem uncannily dark.

'How dare he take Bea! How *dare* he!' Susannah had been saying this – or versions of it – since leaving Mistress Cary's, where a bowl of stew and Ellen's remaining spare gown had revived her. 'If he so much as harms a hair on her head, I'll march him to the highest court in the land!'

She was still convinced she could knock on his door and demand her sister's safe return. I didn't dare tell her that in her white cap and plain blue gown, she looked like any other village girl.

Though my plan wasn't much cleverer: I'd assumed we could hop over the wall and sneak in through the kitchen when the maids were elsewhere. That idea was promptly dashed when we saw Dr Blood's dogs. There were four of them, the size of bull calves, roaming loose in the garden. They smelt us even before they'd seen us, and hurled themselves at the wall. It made me jump out of my skin. When a maid came outside to investigate the barking, we ducked behind the nearest tree.

'Your next bright idea, please?' Susannah asked, when the maid had gone inside again, and the dogs calmed down.

I didn't have one. What made it worse was hearing Bea, shouting and screeching, inside the house. We could see maids moving in front of the windows, passing a baby between them. It was awful knowing we couldn't help.

'Oh, I wish they could settle her,' Susannah fretted.

'If they just rubbed her back and blew on her face,' I agreed. 'She likes that.'

'I thought you weren't fond of babies.'

'I'm fond of Bea. She can say my name, you know.'

Susannah tried not to smile.

*

We watched the house for an hour or more. The maids kept walking Bea to and fro, though it didn't do much good. She had stamina, did Bea, when it came to yelling. And from the speed with which each maid was passing her on to the next, it was obvious they were getting fed up. I counted four maids in total. The smoke coming from the chimneys was a sign that Dr Blood was also at home: this was confirmed when we finally heard him shout, 'FOR HEAVEN'S SAKE, WILL SOMEONE QUIETEN THAT BABY!'

'Perhaps he should get off his backside and try,' Susannah muttered crossly.

I'd not heard her say such a coarse word before, but it got me thinking. What if Dr Blood *did* have to take care of Bea, all by himself? He was keen enough to snatch her from me, so perhaps he should have a taste of what he'd taken on – a real taste, not the half-measures kind where four maids were doing the hard work for him.

*

A short while later we'd agreed on a new plan. It involved chicken carcasses and lies – lots of lies – about a pedlar making it through the floods somehow and arriving in Glastonbury with ribbons to sell, and soap, and perhaps even some sugar, and how everyone was rushing to buy what he had. This was Susannah's idea, because she said no one could resist nice things when they knew everyone else wanted them. Which was a little how it was with the crewel-work piece.

'You have still got it?' I asked.

She patted her sleeve, which on Ellen's dress was wider than her nightgown had been, so I advised her to tuck it up past the elbow.

'Just in case of thieves,' I said, knowingly.

'You've never had anything stolen, have you?'

'Once. At the hiring fair.' I felt a prickle of anger, recalling it. 'That woman who nearly hired me before your father came along.'

Susannah looked thoughtful. 'Hmmm, I remember. Though I don't believe she was stealing from you.'

'She ran off with a parcel my mother gave me,' I insisted. 'I'd call that thieving.'

She shrugged. 'It looked to me as if she'd taken fright at something.'

'What, *Maira*?' I wasn't convinced. The woman I remembered didn't look the type to be scared of anything – or anyone.

Susannah was on her feet, brushing dead leaves off her skirts.

'Come,' she said. 'We've a baby to rescue.'

*

The chicken carcasses came from the nearest ale house. I crept into the back kitchen when no one was looking, and took as many as I could carry from the pile waiting for the cooking pot. Back at Dr Blood's I lobbed a couple over the wall. Just as I'd hoped, the dogs went crazy and were so busy fighting over them, Susannah was able to dash up the path unnoticed.

I watched with baited breath as she knocked on the door. Having never understood the lure of soap or ribbons, I wasn't entirely convinced the ruse would work. But Susannah, with her expensive voice, quickly captured the maids' interest. Or maybe it was the result of a morning with a squawking baby, and they couldn't wait to leave the house.

'Dr Blood's not happy. I heard him shouting,' Susannah whispered, once she'd joined me behind the tree again.

'Good. That's the plan.'

Moments later, the door opened, and the maids, baskets tucked under their arms, hurried down the path.

'I FORBID YOU TO GO. COME BACK AT ONCE!' roared a voice from inside.

The last maid, giggling, pulled the door shut behind her. They disappeared off down the lane.

'How long do we wait?' Susannah asked.

'Until he cracks and comes out.'

We watched the house. I chewed the skin round my fingers. Susannah sucked an end of her hair.

From inside, Bea's faint cries could still be heard. This time no one walked her up and down at the window. It was getting harder to listen, to be honest, thinking she'd just been left to sob her heart out.

Susannah stood up.

'I can't bear it any more,' she said. 'I'm going to get her.'

She hadn't taken a step when the front door flew open.

'Get down!' I hissed.

She dropped to a crouch again as Dr Blood came storming down the path in his shirtsleeves. Bea wasn't with him: it was exactly as I'd hoped.

'Can't be expected to work in these conditions . . .' he was muttering. 'Any more of that racket and I'll go mad . . .'

The dogs ran up to him in greeting, but he pushed them away, charged out of the gate and went after the maids.

I met Susannah's eye. 'Now?'

She nodded.

The remaining chicken carcasses went over the

wall first, us following quickly behind. We sprinted up the path. The front door was unlocked, but stiff. I shouldered it open and we rushed in. The house was stuffy, smelling of smoke and roasting meat, and though Bea had been in here howling, she certainly wasn't now. It was deadly quiet.

'Try the kitchen,' I told Susannah. 'I'll look in the upstairs parlour.'

There was nothing there but a cat fast asleep in a chair. Starting to panic, I ran back downstairs, almost straight into Susannah.

'Look who I found,' she said.

Bea, red-faced and wet-eyed, was gazing up at her sister. I nearly sobbed myself with relief.

'We need to hurry,' I warned. 'Those chicken carcasses won't last long.'

As it was, they were gone, entirely. The dogs' heads were up: they'd smelt us and were interested. We pelted down the path, as fast as anyone could in long skirts, the dogs giving chase. I reached the wall first and vaulted over. The pain in my rib made me yelp.

'Quick! Take her!' Susannah cried, handing me Bea.

She scrambled over the wall, kicking at the dogs as they leaped for her feet. And then she was over, landing awkwardly beside me.

We grinned at each other. We'd done it. Bea clutched her sister's hair and giggled.

As we started walking, Susannah checked her sleeve again for the crewel work. The frown on her face made me stop.

'It's not there, is it?' I said, dread upon me.

She shook out her arm frantically.

'I had it, I swear I did,' she cried.

But we both knew the full horror of what had happened: she'd dropped it inside the house.

21

We couldn't go back for the crewel work. Behind Dr Blood's wall, the dogs were yammering. And in the other direction coming up the lane were the maids, swinging their empty baskets and arguing amongst themselves. Dr Blood was there too, looking the most furious of the lot.

'Quick! Get down!' I pulled Susannah and Bea behind a nearby woodpile.

'That baby might mean nothing to any of you slatterns,' Dr Blood was fuming as he went by, 'but she's currently my most valuable asset.'

'And we're only saying, sir,' one of the maids protested, 'that we were told in good faith of a pedlar come to town. The girl who said so had breeding, so she did.'

'What *girl*?' Dr Blood demanded.

But they'd hurried past before I could catch the answer.

'We'd better get out of here,' I said, scrambling to my feet.

I wasn't much worried about him discovering Bea was missing – to be honest, he'd probably be glad. It was the likelihood of him finding the crewel work bothered me, and realising it depicted an enormous, terrifying wave, of exactly the kind that had flooded most of coastal Somerset.

If he wanted King James's interest, this would get it. It would also, surely, seal Susannah's fate.

*

We hurried down the track as far as it would take us. It was starting to rain – nasty, sleety stuff driven sideways on a bitter wind. By my reckoning, it was only just past midday, but already the light was dim, leaching colour out of everything. It was hard to believe that what lay sullen and brown in the fields all around us was water from my beloved sea.

By the time we reached the church tower on the hilltop, we were being followed. I felt a surge of panic. Dr Blood had found the crewel work – and us – a bit too quickly. To make matters worse, he had a group of men with him, villagers probably, who'd know the countryside around here better than we did.

Susannah hadn't noticed yet. She was trying to wrap

Bea in the folds of her dress, and fretting that we'd not thanked Mistress Cary for her kindness when we were still wearing Ellen's two spare gowns.

'It's good manners, Fortune,' she was saying. 'They'll think we're unprincipled thieves.'

I nudged her to look over her shoulder. 'Better that than a witch.'

Dr Blood and the men were gaining on us. They were carrying sticks and pitchforks.

We started running. On the hillside itself, the track split in many directions. I picked one that dipped out of sight around the back of the church, beckoning Susannah to follow: if we were quick then the building might give us a bit of cover.

At ground level there wasn't much to hide behind. The tower was open on all sides to the weather: rain was now streaming in. There was no roof, either, or windows in the arched frames. But there were shallow footholds in the wall.

'We're not, are we?' Susannah looked at me, aghast.

I checked outside: Dr Blood hadn't yet reached the split in the track. But he wasn't far behind.

'If he can't see us, he'll run straight past,' I tried to persuade her. 'It's either climb the tower or hand ourselves over.'

'Just don't go too high up,' Susannah warned me.

Bea gave a little grumble in protest.

Tucking my skirt between my legs, I went first to prove it could be done. The stone was rough against my fingers and shins, but the holds were well spaced: I probably wasn't the first person to hide up here. About ten yards from the ground was a stone ledge. It ran underneath a small window and was just about big enough for us to sit on.

'It's not too bad if you keep close to the wall,' I told Susannah.

She was frowning with concentration, and her climb was painfully slow. It was so much harder with Bea, who kept trying to grab everything. And when I reached down to help, we very nearly lost our balance and went crashing to the ground. Susannah made better progress by herself. All the time, I kept my ears pricked for Dr Blood. Just as Susannah's fingers felt along the ledge for purchase, I heard his voice on the wind.

'It's blatant witchcraft and now I've proof of it.' He was furious still. 'Our whole county has been overlooked.'

'*Overlooked?*' Susannah heard it too and frowned at me as if she didn't know the word.

I did, and shivered. 'Under a witch's spell, that's what he means.'

We both knew the dropped crewel work was his proof.

Taking her arm, I hauled her up next to me on the ledge. Bea's unhappy face poked out of Susannah's bodice. She was probably hungry, poor thing. I kissed her and promised we'd find her something soon.

Moments later, Dr Blood was inside the church tower. We found ourselves peering down on to the heads of a dozen or so men. They felt dangerously close. I could see the weave of a jacket, the lice in one man's hair. Any of the men would only need to glance up, and they'd discover our hiding place. Susannah wrapped her arms tightly around Bea. I pressed a finger to my mouth: it was vital we kept absolutely silent.

Thankfully, the men were convinced we'd carried on down into the valley.

'We should follow the main track,' a man in a waistcoat was suggesting. 'I s'pect they've gone that way. Floods are shallower down there.'

'I've heard witches don't like water,' said another.

Dr Blood muttered under his breath about the rain. Outside, the weather had worsened, and the men seemed reluctant to go out in it again, lingering under what little shelter the old tower gave. And so we waited. And waited. I dreaded Bea starting to cry or me needing to sneeze.

It was Susannah who made the noise – her heel scraping the stone wall. A shower of dust fell on to the sheltering men's shoulders.

'What was that?' one of them asked.

'Whole place ain't about to come down, is it?' said another.

I didn't see them glance upwards, though they must have. I was twisting round to look out of the window. The drop wasn't more than six or seven feet, since the ground rose up around the church walls. At most we'd turn an ankle, which, to my mind, was worth the risk.

I climbed up on the sill. Swinging myself round, I got my legs out first and shuffled to the edge.

It was now or never.

Yet before I could jump, I was pushed.

'Go!' Susannah hissed.

Arms, legs, barrelled into the back of me, and suddenly we were both falling. I landed badly on my side, the air forced out of my chest. Susannah hit the grass bank then rolled into a nearby hedge.

I crawled over to her. Bea was fine and blew dribble

in my face. But the fact Susannah was still sitting on the ground wasn't a good sign.

'Come on!' I cried, grabbing her arm.

'I can't move! Ouch, don't pull me!'

The men were spilling out of the church, bewildered as to where we'd gone. We had seconds at most before they spotted us.

'What's hurting?' I demanded.

She pointed frantically to her head. 'My hair. It's caught in the hedge.'

It really was too. Her cap had come off in the fall, and now the knotted mess of hair and hawthorn held her as fast as a gaoler's rope. The only way we'd get her out was to cut her free.

'I'll find a flint,' I told her. 'Stay still.'

But there weren't any flints, and the men were coming around the side of the church. I crouched in front of Susannah and took both of her hands.

'I need you to be brave,' I said.

She gulped.

'On the count of three, I'm going to pull you up and you must push,' I told her. 'It'll hurt but it'll be quick.'

I felt bad at asking her to do something painful. My only hope was that her hair was brittle like mine and would snap when we pulled.

Yet before I could count, Susannah got up so fast she almost knocked me off my feet. Her head was yanked back. Another wrench. A snapping of twigs. And she tripped into me, free.

I didn't look back to see how close the men were. Or how much of Susannah's hair we'd left hanging in the hedge like Old Man's Beard. All we could do was run.

22

We raced downhill, crashing through undergrowth, ditches, across the flood where it was shallow enough to wade. Ellen's skirts, too long for running, kept tripping me up. I'd have given my right arm for a pair of leggings. Susannah had a technique of wrapping her hems around her wrist to keep them out of the way, which made me wonder how often she'd run across country. She was as fast as a hound.

Yet there came a point where we had to slow down. Both of us were seriously out of breath, and poor Bea was crying. She'd been sick all down Susannah's front.

'She needs to eat,' Susannah gasped, holding her side. 'And to rest. As do I.'

I was about to point out that food wouldn't magically appear at the ring of a servant's bell, when I noticed we'd shaken off our followers. I didn't trust the situation; they'd catch us up soon enough. But we did need a breather, and since we were approaching a farmstead, it seemed as good a time as any to rest.

'Only a short stop, mind,' I warned Susannah. 'No falling asleep.'

The farm had been completely flooded out. Doors and windows stood open, and the yard was crammed with chairs and boxes, a cabinet floating on its back. There was no sign of anyone here, and to be honest, I didn't search too hard, fearful of what I might see.

We found a hayloft that looked dry, at least, and while Susannah climbed up to it, I went to find food. All I came upon was a single sheep, penned in by water at the back of a barn. Luckily it had plenty to eat, and better still, it was bursting to be milked.

Back at the hayloft, Susannah was waiting hungrily. In the last of the day's light, I could see the spot by her ear where a chunk of hair was missing. Other than that the hedge incident had left her unscathed, though she wrinkled her nose when I passed her the bucket of milk.

'This came from a *sheep*?' she said in disbelief.

Bea wasn't so fussy. She drank plenty of the sheep's milk, and once we'd cleaned her up with handfuls of hay, she stretched her arms behind her head and fell asleep. I gulped down my share of the milk. It was still warm, with a rich, salty taste.

'Here,' I tried again to give the bucket to Susannah. 'It's delicious.'

Susannah took the milk. She sniffed it. Sipped it. Pulled a face.

'Anyone would think it was the chamber pot I'd offered you!' I cried.

Pinching her nose, she downed the remaining milk.

'Happy now?' she gasped, all triumphant. There was milk on her top lip and she belched into the back of her hand. The look of her made it hard not to laugh, and I almost did until she said, 'You're not serious about returning to your village, are you?'

I straightened up. 'Of course I am. And you're coming with me.'

'I don't think so, Fortune,' she replied. 'That is very generous of you, but I need to know what's happened to Ellis. If he's still alive then mine and Bea's lives should be with him.'

I thought of Berrow Hall, the smashed windows, the torn-off doors, the whole house full of water.

'Do you suppose Berrow Hall is still standing?' I asked.

'Probably not,' she admitted. 'And good riddance to the place. I don't wish to live there again, but the land will still be ours. We'll have to do something with it; it's a huge estate – twenty miles wide, to be precise.'

I whistled. It made Old Margaret's land – and that of our neighbours – seem like little herb gardens in comparison.

'Not forgetting,' Susannah added, 'Ellis is mine and Bea's brother. I do want to be part of a family again.'

'Then come and join mine until you find yours,' I begged. 'Please. I promise you'll be safe.'

'Without wishing to offend, what would I *do* in a village like yours?'

'Actually, it's a hamlet,' I admitted.

'Exactly. I'd be useless. I can't chop wood, I can't cook, I didn't even know you could milk a sheep!'

'But you'll learn,' I told her. 'You'll have to. That old life of yours has gone, at least while Dr Blood is still after you.'

'And Bea?'

'Of course she's welcome!' I insisted. The thought of not seeing Bea every day made me panic slightly. 'You'll be as safe with us as anywhere. The witch hunters came once but they've not been back, not since we put my brother in charge.'

Susannah smoothed the folds of her skirts, thinking.

Questions slid into my brain too. What would it

be like, going back to Fair Maidens Lane? Would the flood have damaged it? Would my family be all right? Might Jem still be cross with me? It certainly wasn't the homecoming I'd hoped for, where I'd be swanking home with a purse of coins. I'd no wages to speak of, nor did I still have Mother's gift.

'Very well,' Susannah said eventually. 'And thank you, Fortune.' She was trying hard not to cry.

*

Despite my warning, we did both fall asleep. It was dark when we woke up, and so cold our breath came out like smoke. I was worried we'd climb down from the hayloft to find Dr Blood waiting, but what greeted us instead was an uncanny quiet. Wrapping up a very sleepy Bea, we headed out into the dark to walk further along the valley. I kept my eyes peeled for a place to cross the floods, being certain that, from the stars, Fair Maidens Lane lay to our west.

The flood quickly got deeper. It was hard to see how far ahead the water stretched, but I felt the chill coming off it like mist.

'We'll swim if we have to,' I said, bracing myself.

Susannah went silent – a tense, shivery sort of

silence that told me she was scared. It reminded me of Jem, that day in the boat, when we'd drifted into too-deep water.

'You can't swim, can you?' I asked.

'No. I can't.' She glanced at me. 'Why, can you?'

'I haven't drowned yet, put it that way.'

But I couldn't swim for all of us, that I did know. In water this cold, it'd be hard enough keeping myself afloat, never mind with a girl and a baby in tow.

'We could wait until morning?' Susannah suggested.

I shook my head. It would mean wasting more time, and for a while now we'd been trailed by the faintest of noises – rustling grass, twigs snapping. It might've been badgers, or a night-time breeze. But I wasn't convinced.

'There must be another way through the water,' I said, scanning the dark. 'A bridge, a wall – can you see anything?'

'No. Not a thing.'

Behind us, a squelching sound. Boots moving through mud.

Susannah gripped my arm. I turned slowly. The trees were shaking, whispering. Overhead, an owl screeched. It came again, the sticky slurp of muddy footsteps.

Someone was coming towards us.

'Keep hold of my arm,' I whispered. 'We're going to start walking again,' because I couldn't think what else to do.

23

As silent as snakes, we slid into the water. The cold of it was so shocking I had to fight the urge to yelp. Susannah's fingers dug into my arm as the floods reached our shins, our knees. Once or twice, when I felt her hesitate, I urged her on. Before long, the quiet seemed to settle again, Susannah's chattering teeth the only noise I could hear.

'I think we've lost them,' I whispered.

'Dr Blood is a plump coward,' she whispered back. 'He'd never keep up with us for long.'

Still, we didn't dare stop. We crossed one field, then another, this time wading downhill. Overhead, the cloud had thinned to reveal an almost-full moon, which lit up the floods ahead of us with a silvery path. The water began to deepen, until it was up to our hips. Beneath the surface, things brushed against my legs. I tried to believe they were just sticks or old cabbage stalks, but my exhausted brain kept tricking me into remembering all the dead creatures I'd seen these past couple of days. I wasn't convinced we'd lost Dr Blood for good, either. Every hedgerow, every man-shaped tree made me start. Susannah was as jumpy as I was, and suddenly stopped dead. 'Lord above, look at that, would you?'

'What is it?' I hissed, my heart beating very fast.

She let go of my hand to point. 'Over there. It's a living animal – is it a cow?'

As my eyes adjusted, I saw steam coming from the creature's nostrils, and the curve of a pair of very pricked ears.

'It's a *horse*!' I almost laughed in relief.

The poor thing was standing in the small part of the field where the water was at its shallowest. It whinnied, sounding as relieved as I was. Before we knew it, it was coming towards us. It wasn't a small beast, either, and its big chest pushing against the water sent little waves that broke on us, splashing our faces.

I was a bit wary of horses, to be honest, but when it reached us, it stopped, sniffed us very gently, then rested its hairy chin on my shoulder. Bea squealed in delight and tried to grab its mane.

'Dear creature, it's so pleased to see someone,' Susannah crooned, stroking its nose.

'It wants us to rescue it,' I guessed.

'Can't we?'

I thought she was joking.

'Horses are great swimmers,' she explained. 'And look at her, she's got a back wide enough for all of us.'

'You mean, we ride the horse through the water?' I said, because it honestly hadn't occurred to me.

*

It wasn't exactly comfortable, sitting astride the horse, but Susannah was in front of me, so she could tell the creature what to do.

I wrapped my arms tightly around her waist, just below the bump in her bodice made by Bea, who, now she actually needed to hold the horse's mane, was trying to eat her sister's hair instead.

'Ready?' Susannah asked.

I grimaced. 'As I'll ever be.' In truth, I felt a bit sorry for the poor beast who had two dripping-wet people to carry.

Yet carry us she did, with long easy strides that took us across the valley in very little time. We struck out along a road – at least, it seemed like one, for buildings ran along it on either side. There were no lamps at the windows though, or smoking chimneys or barking dogs tied up in the yards. The only sound was the lap of water. It might've been restful on a beach or by a river, but here it felt strange and haunting. We passed flood-filled barns, where hay meant for the animals now floated in mouldering heaps, and houses with their front doors warped.

'Where is everyone?' Susannah wondered out loud.

I kept quiet. I was thinking of drowned bodies again, and of my family, who I prayed were safe: seeing all these damaged homes was making me worry. Susannah, I sensed, was thinking of Ellis. At least, something had made her gentle shivering suddenly stop, then start again as a violent shudder. It was difficult to keep my arms round her.

'What's the matter?' I asked.

With difficulty, she untangled her fingers from the horse's thick mane, and pointed not far ahead where the houses stopped. Beyond it, the water waited like a threat.

'It gets deep again,' Susannah warned.

'You said horses could swim,' I reminded her.

She squared her shoulders. 'So I did.'

A squeeze from her heels and the horse broke into a trot. I really did have to hold on with all my strength now, yet still seemed be slipping one way, then the other, but always in the direction of the horse's belly. The bones in my backside hurt. As for my legs, I'd stopped feeling them a few miles ago.

We hit the water at speed. The horse surged forward like a boat launching, then suddenly the movement changed. It wasn't a jolting, tooth-rattling trot any more, but something smooth, almost floaty.

'Is this it? Are we swimming?' I asked in amazement.

'We are. Just keep still. Let her find her way.'

The horse seemed to be following the line of the trees on our left. Beneath me I could feel its shoulder muscles powering through the water.

'Good girl,' Susannah murmured. 'Queen of horses, that's it.'

The horse, ears flicking at her voice, kept swimming. The water lapped against our legs, but came up no higher, which meant Bea, at least, was snug and dry. We were gliding so effortlessly, I began to relax. It reminded me of floating in the boat with Jem, when I'd been so at peace. I laid my cheek against Susannah's shoulder, feeling the warmth of her through her dress. The horse's gentle movement went on: I was so tired I couldn't help but close my eyes.

When I came to, we were on dry land again, no

longer moving. The horse was snorting and shaking its head. Susannah's shoulder blades beneath my cheek felt tense.

'What's happened?' I asked, blinking awake. There was too much light to see properly what was going on.

Susannah didn't reply. The light, I realised in horror, came from burning torches. We were surrounded on all sides. The witch-hunt had caught us.

IV

IN WHICH OUR HERO BELIEVES HER LUCK IS CHANGING AT LAST

24

'By my word, if it isn't Fortune Sharpe!'

I was stunned to hear my name, not Susannah's.

'Who's asking?' I wanted to know: the torches were so bright I couldn't see beyond them.

'I should've guessed you'd survive such a catastrophic flood,' the person replied.

Odd, but I recognised the voice – a woman's. The rolled 'r's were like our local accent, only warmer.

'Do you know her?' Susannah whispered. 'Because she seems to know you.'

The torches parted. A figure came towards us, laying her hand gently on the horse's shoulder. The face looking up at me was dark and strong, and one I'd not expected to see again.

Maira.

'You!' I spluttered.

At the exact same moment Susannah nudged me. 'It's the woman from the hiring fair!'

Maira took in our wet skirts, plastered against the horse's flanks. Her mouth twitched into a smile. 'Oh, dear child. You were so much more use to me in breeches.'

But I was already sliding off the horse, determined to prove that wearing a girl's clothes didn't make me useless. My legs had other plans. As I hit the ground, I swayed dizzily. Maira caught me by the elbow and set me back on my feet.

The torches closed in around us. Now my eyes had adjusted I could see faces, all dark like Maira's, staring at us with interest. I bet we did look a sight, mind you, two soaked-to-the-bone girls and a baby, wide awake, trying to squirm out of the front of Susannah's dress.

'Your ranks have grown since we last met,' Maira observed.

'These are my friends, yes.' I was wary. Despite Susannah's view of why Maira had vanished with Mother's parcel, I still wasn't entirely convinced she hadn't thieved from me.

'Hmmm . . . and I'd say you're in some sort of trouble, am I right?' Maira asked.

I bit my lip. Could I tell her? Could I trust the feeling I had standing before her, the awe, the flutter in the pit of my stomach? Even now I wondered what my life would have been like if she'd hired me that day at the fair.

'Fwwwwafwwaaa! Waaaannnnt!' Bea yelled.

One of the torch carriers – a boy near my age, I'd guess – was pulling silly faces at her. It set Bea off, giggling and reaching out to him. Maybe it was a sign that these were decent people after all – wasn't Bea supposed to have a knack for knowing?

Susannah certainly seemed to think so. Before I'd a chance to speak again, she was telling Maira about our situation.

'We're currently being followed, I'm afraid,' she admitted, 'by a man who thinks I'm a witch.'

'*You?* Ha!' Maira laughed. I don't think she'd seen a more unlikely witch in her life. 'Then you'd best hide with us tonight, hadn't you? I hope you'll like our boat.'

*

I thought she was joking or that I'd misheard her. Yet after a short walk through a soggy-underfoot meadow, we came to the boat in question. It wasn't huge, but clearly it had a crew and a hull and a sail that hung limply from its mast. It was also about two miles from the sea, on its side in a field, which was good news for the horse, at least, who soon had her head down in the grass.

Maira's boat was called the *Songbird*, and had a gash in its hull, just above where its name was painted in swirly letters. The hole had to be fixed before the boat could be seaworthy again.

'In the harbour we were, moored to an iron ring this big . . . ' Maira held her hands apart. 'That strange old wave tore us from the harbour wall.'

'You're a *sailor*!' I realised.

So this was the work she'd wanted me for. If it hadn't been for Mr Spicer butting in, I'd have joined her too, and spent these past few weeks sailing the ocean as one of her crew. I felt stung that I'd missed out on such a chance. Though if I'd gone with Maira I'd never have met Ellis and Susannah, and Bea, and I wouldn't have wanted that, either.

Maira and her crew clambered on to the boat, then reached down to help us. Someone grabbed the back of my gown, hauling me off the ground. I scrambled the rest of the way, and when my feet landed on the slippery, sloping deck, I couldn't help but grin. For the first time in my life I was on a proper boat. If only Jem could see me now!

Maira, opening the hatch, quickly ordered us all

below deck. The flaming torches were replaced with a couple of little yellow-glass lanterns. One by one, we climbed down a ladder into the gloom.

'No witch hunters are welcome here,' Maira declared, bolting the hatch behind us.

Below deck, the air felt as warm and close as being underneath a blanket. The ceiling was so low you had to crouch when you walked – not that there was far to go. The whole living space looked no bigger than two or three horse stalls. Everywhere was wood – wood ceilings, wood walls, great beams running across and down into the floor. At one end of the boat were hammocks, clothes on hooks, jars and baskets of supplies tied to shelves. At the other, a couple of trunks, some rope, a small firebox for cooking. Though everything was on a perilous slant, it felt as safe as an animal's burrow. Already I could feel my shoulders dropping, my thoughts untangling.

For the second time in as many days, we were given dry clothes – not women's clothes, thankfully, but shirts, jackets and breeches the same as the rest of the crew wore.

The face-pulling boy was called Pepper.

'Mine from long ago,' he said, handing Susannah a tiny wool vest. 'For the little one.'

The vest was huge on Bea, and she'd soon squirmed

free of it to crawl between legs and climb on to laps. But Susannah was smiling, thanking Pepper, thanking Maira.

'What a stroke of luck to find these people,' she said quietly in my ear.

In fact, they'd found us. In the soft light of the lanterns, I was able to get a better look at Maira's crew. They were a team of four: two girls, Pepper and another boy, all older than us, and with exciting names. Pepper had beautiful ink drawings on his arms. Rex carried the ship's tabby cat on his shoulder like a bird. The girls, Flint and Arrow, wore single gold earrings, and were strong and quick. I couldn't help but wonder what Maira had seen in me that day, what my part would've been in a team like this.

The crew deferred to Maira like she was royalty. Susannah kept whispering that it was ill-mannered of me to stare, though she was doing the same.

'She looks very dashing in breeches,' Susannah murmured.

'She's also captain of this ship,' I pointed out, because even I, who'd been raised by capable women, hadn't known such a thing was possible. It was another reason to be impressed by Maira.

While Bea sucked the honey from a piece of bread,

Arrow fed us hard biscuits and strips of meat so salty it made me cough. Afterwards, we drank beer and wrapped ourselves in blankets that smelled of salt and sunshine. I began imagining what it would be like to do this every night, with the sway of the sea beneath us.

And it wasn't that difficult. I'd a feeling I could be myself amongst these people. In fact, I'd bet a silver coin Maira and her crew knew what it was like to be stared at, talked about for being different. On board the boat, they were free of all that. They could be who *they* wanted to be. To live a life with no boring household tasks, no long skirts, no expectation to be virtuous and quiet. What's more, they'd see the sea every single day. If Maira had hired me this would've been my life, and I would've fitted in here. But we were past all that now, I realised sadly.

Susannah, meanwhile, was fretting over our discarded gowns.

'We really should return Ellen's clothes to her,' she said. 'She only had three dresses, and we took two of them.'

'I'm not going back to Glastonbury, not for anyone,' I replied with a shudder.

'They'll need mending, anyway. Mine's ripped.'

While Pepper sorted her out with sewing things

and a lantern, I settled back on the floor, cradling Bea in my lap. We all fell into an easy, drowsy silence. One by one people crawled off to their hammocks to sleep, until Susannah returned to claim Bea, who was now snoring gently. That left just me and Maira.

I knew I had to ask her what had happened to Mother's parcel; all evening I'd been mulling over when to, and how. As it was, she beat me to it, pulling the package from her jacket.

'I never intended to take it from you,' she said, placing it in my hands and closing them around it like a shell. 'But I knew you'd come back for it, Fortune Sharpe.'

So she hadn't thieved it. I wasn't sure what pleased me more: having the package returned, or being able to now fully trust this person I admired. And the truth was if she'd not taken it, it would've likely been lost in the flood anyway.

'Thank you.' I'd tears in my eyes. 'My mother gave it to me just before we parted company.'

Maira had looked after it well. The fabric was neatly folded, the dried skin inside still in one wizened piece.

'Do you know what it is now?' she asked.

'Umm … not really,' I admitted.

'It's a caul. You were born with it covering your head.'

'I was?' I stared at it, thinking what a strange, ugly thing it was to give as a gift. 'My mother kept it all this time?'

'Of course she did. She knew how auspicious it was. Being born with a caul brings great protection, child, because it means you'll never drown.'

'I *can* swim a bit, actually,' I pointed out.

'Ah, yet even the strongest swimmers can drown. Amongst sailors and seafaring folk, a caul is a very lucky object. You're not simply Fortune in name, you know.'

I turned over the piece of skin in my hands. Back home it was Jem who'd been the special one; this caul was something that marked me out too. I supposed it might explain why I loved the sea so much, why going out in our makeshift boat that day hadn't scared me.

'Did the caul help me survive the flood, do you think?' I asked.

'Maybe.' Maira shrugged. 'It was certainly why I wanted to hire you that day in Bridgwater.'

'Then why didn't you?'

She thought for a moment. 'You weren't ready.'

'I would've been,' I insisted.

'No, you weren't. But I believe you are now.'

I looked at her. Her eyes were very deep and dark.

'Would you come to sea with us now, Fortune Sharpe, if I asked you?' she asked.

I felt that flutter again, in the pit of my stomach. Me, a crew member, like Pepper and the others, with my own hammock to sleep in? A life of freedom, of wearing breeches, of being myself? Did Maira mean it? The look on her face told me she did.

I took a long breath.

'I made a promise to Susannah that she could stay with me and my family,' I replied. 'I can't let her down. I'm sorry.'

Maira nodded. 'We leave from Withy Cove, about two miles down the coast, at sundown tomorrow – at least that is our aim.'

'But I can't come,' I tried to explain. 'I'm sorry. I've—'

She held up her hand. 'So you've already told me.'

But the questions, the 'what ifs', were unfurling inside my head. And Maira knew it as well as I did.

25

The next morning, we set off with the risen sun behind us. It was a wrench saying goodbye to the *Songbird* and her crew, yet as much as I was tempted by Maira's offer, I was still resolved to help Susannah and Bea. There was also the small fact of my own dear family who I was eager as anything to see again.

The horse, whom Susannah named Blaze on account of the white stripe on her face, came with us. We'd tried to turn her loose, but she followed us down the lane, so in the end Maira fashioned a halter from rope and begged us to take her.

'What use have we for a horse on a ship?' she said, which was a fair point.

Susannah wanted to ride Blaze, but I preferred to walk. It was a good arrangement for it meant we could both keep an eye out for anyone who might be following us or acting suspiciously. Despite the odd knee-deep stretch of lying water or thick mud, there was no need for anyone – girl or horse – to swim.

Bea, secure in a new sling across Susannah's chest, loved it up on Blaze, and was talking and pointing at everything we passed. I felt in reasonable spirits too. Mother's parcel had been safely returned to me and was tucked inside my shirt. And this morning's brisk walk was so much easier in sailor's breeches.

After another few miles with no sign of Dr Blood, my mind drifted to Jem, Mother and Abigail, and how much I'd missed them all. I couldn't wait for them to meet Susannah and Bea, and I hoped they'd find a use for Blaze. Meanwhile, Susannah had gone very quiet.

In the end, I asked her what was wrong.

'It's your poor family I'm worried about,' Susannah replied. 'How can you be sure they've not been flooded when so many have?'

I explained that Fair Maidens Lane was sheltered from the sea by a steep hill.

'The flood mightn't have even reached them,' I tried to assure her. 'And if it did, it probably hasn't done too much damage.'

We walked on. The heavy silence still hung over her, making me think the matter wasn't closed. She'd also insisted on bringing Ellen's gowns to return, and carried them in a bundle on her hip, which she'd started fidgeting with. Eventually, the bundle slid to the ground.

'Shall I carry it?' I offered.

'I have to tell you something!' she burst out.

I stopped and looked up at her.

'When I sewed Ellen's dress last night . . . the needle and thread . . . it happened again.'

'Oh mercy!' I muttered. 'What was it this time?'

'Terrible things happening to you, Fortune,' she cried. 'Something to do with water and drowning.'

But that couldn't be right, could it? After what Maira had told me last night, then surely this was one prediction that wouldn't come true.

'Why are you smiling?' Susannah said crossly.

I squeezed her dangling foot. 'Because it's all right, nothing bad will happen to me, I promise. Maira told me—'

'Told you what?'

'That parcel of mine she took? It was a caul. I was born with it covering my head.'

She blinked in surprise. 'Oh, which means you'll never drown, and you'll bring good luck to sailors, isn't that right?'

'Something like that.' I nodded. 'So forget what your needle and thread told you. It won't happen.'

'I'm not a witch then, despite what Dr Blood might think?'

'I don't care what he thinks: do you?'

Susannah wiped her face. Shook her head. After a moment, she said, 'What *is* a witch, anyway?'

I thought about it.

'A clever woman,' I decided, 'who knows her own mind.'

'You don't believe it's about magic?'

I shrugged. 'Maybe. But doesn't everyone have a bit of strangeness in them? Imagine how dull life would be if we could explain every single little thing.'

'Yaaaaaa!' said Bea, who agreed.

*

As the road took us further inland, we passed farmsteads where people were sweeping the last of the water out of their yards. Animals were feeding, a man was fixing a gate, two women were beating a carpet hung on a line. On the banks of the lanes, the first snowdrops were trying to appear. It could have been any winter's day here in Somerset, and was all heartening evidence that normal life was returning.

Better still was when we reached a fork in the road. There on the milestone was the name of Nether Stowey, our nearest town. On recognising the symbols, I could've cried for joy.

We were only four sweet, easy miles from Fair Maidens Lane. We'd be home in less than a couple of hours.

I began to tell Susannah about my family – how Jem snored though insisted he didn't, and that Mother made the most delicious oatcakes on the griddle over the fire.

'You'll find Abigail ...' I searched for the word, '*disapproving*, sometimes.'

Susannah listened closely, taking it all in.

Before long we were on the same road I'd travelled with Mother that night in December. It ran straight as a table's edge, with banks of willow trees on either side: beyond it, the fields still lay underwater. Whether that was the result of the big flood or the usual winter rains I couldn't tell, only that the ice had now gone, and the wind rippled across the surface, making the water dance like a little sea.

Everything was recognisable yet different: maybe I

was too. I wondered what my family would think when they saw me. Would Jem say I'd grown? Would Mother and Abigail tut at my sailor's clothes? Would they fall in love with Bea, as I had done? And what of Susannah? In a hamlet of strong-minded women, I hoped she'd find a way to fit in.

*

The town was busy when we reached it. It was market day, though there didn't seem to be much selling going on. Most of the fare laid out on stalls looked pretty meagre – old turnips, sacks of damp flour, a few scrawny chickens, powder-dry herbs. The snowdrops might be coming up, but it would take weeks – maybe months – before the land recovered fully. That was the reality. In our family, Jem and Abigail were both big eaters and I dearly hoped they were managing all right.

Past the church, we joined the main street, which was choked with farm carts and knots of people gathered on the roadside to talk. It wasn't anything unusual for a market day, where gossip was just something else to trade. It was when we stopped at the water trough for Blaze to drink that I overheard a man mention the king.

'He'll arrive from London in a couple of days, roads permitting,' the man said.

'Wants to see the flood damage, does he?' replied the woman he was talking to. 'He could come and stay at my house – if I still had one.'

Her friend laughed bitterly. "Tis why there's nothing decent on sale today. It's all been kept back to feed King James.'

A dairymaid, carrying a yoke across her shoulders, agreed it was. 'We had to save our best cheeses, and stamp our fresh butter with the royal crest.'

'If we don't make him welcome, it's treason. That's the law,' the woman with no house pointed out.

These people looked unimpressed.

'Who's invited his Royal Highness?' someone else asked.

'That Dr Blood, the tooth-barber from Glastonbury,' the man said. 'The king wants justice, so he does, for those who've suffered from this flood.'

All the fear I'd felt yesterday came rushing back. Of course Dr Blood was involved – he was the local magistrate – and this sounded very like the plan I'd heard him speaking about on Twelfth Night.

'So he's putting the sea on trial, is he?' the woman said.

'No, mistress,' the man answered. 'They're saying it's all the work of a cunning woman. Dr Blood's summoned a man from Essex – Mr Hopkins he's called – who's got a reputation for sniffing them out.'

The woman frowned. 'Sniffing *what* out? Cunning?'

'Witches.'

Susannah gave me a warning nudge with her foot.

'That's enough water, guzzle guts,' I said, pulling up Blaze's head.

As we hurried away, neither of us dared say a word.

26

What I'd overheard in town put me in a rare fright. We'd not shaken off Dr Blood, that much was evident. With the king on his way *and* a specialist witch hunter, his mission was, if anything, gathering strength. Nor was it a royal visit to bring charity to our devastated county, it was all about finding someone to blame.

'Dr Blood won't think to search for you in a tiny hamlet,' I tried to reassure Susannah.

'Won't he?' She wasn't convinced. 'Blood by name, blood*hound* by nature.'

If the witch-hunt did track her down to Fair Maidens Lane, then surely Jem would know what to do. I could picture him now, blocking their passage down our narrow path, but doing so politely; reasoning and listening and even shaking hands with Dr Blood if it meant they'd leave us alone. And if that didn't work?

Well, it had to.

Still, I caught myself thinking about Maira's offer

again. They were leaving tonight. We might still make it to Withy Cove. And if she really wanted me and my caul on board, then could I persuade her to take Susannah and Bea? Would Susannah even want to go, when she was set on finding Ellis? It wasn't my finest idea – Susannah couldn't swim, Bea couldn't keep still. We'd have to be desperate.

*

The road out of Nether Stowey was achingly familiar, taking us up the hill before striking north-west across open country towards the coast. What I'd not expected on the high ground was so much lying water. As the road dropped a little towards the sea I was soon wading knee-deep through floodwater again. Bea started to grizzle. And poor Blaze, who for the most part had plodded, as faithful as a dog at my shoulder, was now hesitating.

In my head, I'd assumed the hill would have protected us from the worst of the sea, not like Berrow Hall, which had sat at the top of the beach. But as we walked on, I saw how wrong I'd been. Trees were bent, land waterlogged, roof thatch dripping-wet still and hanging down in clumps. The further we walked, the bleaker it became. There were dead things in ditches, furniture abandoned in the middle of fields where the water had taken it. And the smell – that stagnant, rotten, briny smell – was strong enough to make me retch. Just before the crossroads, a dead sheep floated past. There was a parlour chair stuck in the high branches of an oak tree. A cart overturned in a hedge.

Susannah reached down to squeeze my shoulder.

It'll be all right, that little gesture said, but I didn't think it would be.

My family might not even be alive. And if they were, the last thing they'd need was more mouths to feed, more people to house. I felt suddenly sick with despair.

Up ahead was the left turn for Fair Maidens Lane, and there was our little church peeping above the water. Something odd was on the church roof. At first, it looked like a flock of gulls or roosting doves. But as we got closer I saw they were prayer books, saved from the flood and laid out to dry. I quickened my pace. The memories of long Sunday services spent fidgeting in my dress were all but forgotten. For if the church was still standing then surely the rest of the hamlet would be too.

As we rounded the corner, there was my mother. She was knee-deep in water, arguing with someone I couldn't see properly because the sun was right behind them.

Waving, I called out, 'Mother!'

She spun round.

'Fortune!' she gasped, clutching her throat.

I was ready to run to her, calling Jem's name as well. But the look on her face made me stop. It was an expression I'd never seen before: pleading, terrified, angrier than hell.

'Go!' She came towards me, shooing me away. 'Don't speak to me. Don't look at me. Go!'

I was completely thrown. What on earth had I done wrong?

'But Mother, I've come all this way.' I started to explain about Susannah and Bea, and the kind brown horse they were sitting on.

Abigail appeared, wearing the same baffling expression. 'Get out of here,' my sister hissed. 'And don't come back.'

'What's all this about?' I insisted. 'Where's Jem?'

'He's not here,' she replied, glancing nervously over her shoulder. 'You'd better leave, Fortune, before it's too late.'

The person who'd been arguing with Mother stepped out of the sun. I could see him properly now, for it was a man. He was wearing a black cape, a black doublet straining over his paunch. I felt a stab of fear.

'Fortune Sharpe?' Dr Blood said. 'Just the person I'm looking for.'

Quick as anything, I stood in front of Blaze.

'Get away from us! You're not taking Susannah anywhere!' I cried.

'Do not ill-wish me, child,' Dr Blood warned. 'The evidence is here, look!' In his fist was Susannah's crewel work, showing the sea rearing up, and a boy in a yellow-feathered hat, running away.

'That proves nothing!' I spat. 'You're finding in it what you want to see!'

He took a step towards me. And another.

Mother screamed. 'Don't speak with him, Fortune! Run! RUN!'

It was too late. The fingers of his free hand were closing round my wrist.

'It's not Susannah Spicer we're after,' Dr Blood informed me. 'It's you. It always has been. All I needed was the proof.'

I stared at his hand, damp on my arm. Then at him. His clever ferret eyes. I couldn't believe what I was hearing.

'Me? What've *I* done?' I cried.

I yanked my arm free, but quick as I did so, he grabbed the other one.

'You knew this flood was coming all along,' he said. 'The devil advised you to be prepared, and so you built a boat.'

'That's nonsense!' I replied. And yet, I *had* built a boat, that part was true enough. 'You've been spying on our hamlet!' I cried, remembering the man who watched Jem and me from the clifftop.

'Not me, no,' Dr Blood smiled horribly. 'I paid someone to do it on my behalf.'

The soldier.

'Well, it's all codswallop,' I muttered.

He forced his face close to mine. His breath stank of herrings. 'Is it, now? Let me tell you another of my discoveries. Susannah Spicer's crewel work is dictated by *you*. You're the one who tells her what to sew.'

I gazed at him, stunned. The man was completely mad.

Susannah, meanwhile, had slid down from Blaze. She pushed past me to square up to Dr Blood.

'How dare you speak such utter drivel!' she cried. 'I sew alone, by myself, and always have done. Though why that's any business of yours, I've no idea.'

Dr Blood drew himself up to his full height. 'And yet only when Fortune Sharpe joined your household did you start predicting events. Your dear departed father thought you had a God-given talent, but when he showed me your work I saw how strange it was.'

'What I find *strange*,' Susannah said icily, 'is your need to place the blame of this flood at someone's feet.'

'She's right,' I insisted. 'I haven't done anything wrong.'

'We'll let Mr Hopkins be the judge of that,' he replied. 'Now don't make a fuss. You're coming with us.'

As I struggled, Susannah tried to prise his fingers off my arm.

'You can't take her!' she screamed. 'How dare you!'

Two more dark-cloaked figures waded towards us from the direction of the church. Both had swords and wore the king's emblem at their breasts.

'I am NOT going anywhere!' I kicked up water in Dr Blood's face.

Mother yelled at him to let go of me. One of the soldiers grabbed her arms and pinned them behind her back. Susannah was dragged away, with Bea screaming in her sling. Abigail fell to the ground in tears.

'You'd better take your hands off me, mister!' I cried.

But when I tried to tear myself free again, Dr Blood and more men I didn't recognise blocked my path. I was surrounded by witch hunters.

And that made me the witch.

V

IN WHICH OUR HERO PROTESTS HER INNOCENCE

27

They took me kicking and yelling all the way back to Bridgwater. I didn't remember much of the journey, but I knew that if they'd let go of me for an instant, I'd have run for my life.

In a chamber inside the town hall, two different soldiers took charge of me. Though it was a relief to be rid of Dr Blood, I didn't fancy my chances with these two, either. Both soldiers were as big as bears, with swords like that man on the moors who'd stopped Mother, and it put even more fear into me, thinking they'd readily use them.

'Stop your squirming, brat!' the fiercest soldier growled.

'I'm not a witch!' I protested for the umpteenth time. 'I shouldn't be here!'

'Save your breath for the expert,' Fierce Soldier replied as the chamber door was unlocked. 'This'll be him now.'

The door swung open, admitting a man I didn't recognise. He had something wrong with the left side of his face, like a burn or a birthmark, and wore the cleanest white collar and cuffs I'd ever seen. He didn't introduce himself. But from the fresh panic coursing through me, I guessed he was the famous witch hunter from Essex, Mr Hopkins.

'You must be Fortune Sharpe,' the man said.

'I am, and I'm no witch.'

'Indeed, it is what most of them say,' he replied, not looking at me but at a spot of sunlight on the wall.

'I speak the truth. I'm not a liar.'

Mr Hopkins pursed his lips, pressing his fingertips against them. For one wildly hopeful moment I thought he was considering letting me go.

'Take her down to the strong room,' he said to the soldiers.

The speed of it left me no time to scream. We went along a passageway, down a set of stone steps so fast I tripped over my own feet. The lack of windows and smell of damp told me we were now underneath the town hall. The room we entered had one stool in its centre, and stank of tallow candles and fear. Hands on my shoulders pressed me down on to the seat. The soldiers stood either side of me, Mr Hopkins directly in front.

'You're here on charges of witchcraft,' he said, a long scroll unravelling in his hands. 'Dr Blood tells me you knew the flood was coming months beforehand. That you influenced Susannah Spicer's sewing to cover any suspicions that might arise from your own second sight. And that on the morning of 6th January you did cast a wicked spell on the sea.'

'No!' I insisted. 'None of that is true!'

He glanced up from the scroll. 'I warn you, whatever you say will be written down for the court.'

I breathed through my nose, trying to calm myself. Yet here I was, locked up like a sheep-stealer or a jewel-robber, all because of what the sea had done. Mr Hopkins must be insane to believe what Dr Blood told him. And that was the baffling thing, because he didn't seem mad in the slightest. He spoke gently, politely, much like our curate did if you passed him in the lane.

'The locals say you've always had a close affinity with the sea. Are they right?' Mr Hopkins asked.

I wondered who he'd spoken to: my neighbours? My family? Jem? Any of them might've told him. In Fair Maidens Lane it was common knowledge I loved the beach, though that hardly made me a witch.

He waited for my answer, pen hovering, with the look of someone who had all day. Whereas I didn't. I needed to know my family and friends were safe. Plus, in my panicked brain, Maira's offer was becoming more appealing by the second.

'How long will I be here?' I asked.

'I cannot say.'

'Please, can we hurry?'

Mr Hopkins sighed. Marked something on his paper. Moved down the page. 'Have you ever built a boat?'

I scowled. 'A *what*?'

'A boat,' he repeated patiently. 'The more you tell me, the quicker this will be over.'

And I'd be free to leave, I hoped. Which was all I wanted. I sat a little straighter on the stool.

'Yes,' I said, fighting to keep my voice level. 'I built a boat with my brother Jem, just for a jape. Only a little boat – more of a dugout, really.'

'You were ready for the flood when it arrived, then?'

'Hardly! It let in too much water. It was a pretty useless craft, all told.'

But he didn't seem to be listening. 'Indeed, Dr Blood suggests you had prior knowledge of the flood coming?'

'How? I've never seen a sea like it in my life.'

'But you'd made a boat beforehand,' he insisted. 'Doesn't that strike you as a strange coincidence?'

'I hoped it might be useful for travelling along

the coast. In winter, rain can turn our roads into swamps.'

Mr Hopkins changed tack. 'What age are you, thirteen?'

I was glad of a sensible question.

'Fourteen next year,' I replied. 'Though that depends which calendar you're following.' In the countryside, our year still started the olden way in March, though in the cities it had already changed to begin in January.

Mr Hopkins nodded. He'd written down what he wanted.

'On the sixth day of January, the day of the flood, you were employed at Berrow Hall, as a servant to the son of a Mr Thomas Spicer?' he asked.

I said I was.

'And you were on the beach when the wave struck?'

'Yes, looking for Master Ellis, who we'd reason to believe had run off with a troupe of travelling actors.'

Up until this point the soldiers had been as still as stone. Now one of them sniggered.

Mr Hopkins tutted irritably. 'Tell me about the wave. You saw it first-hand?'

'I did. The sea disappeared completely like you

wouldn't believe. It was all just wet sand. Then it started coming in—'

'Wait,' he interrupted. 'Who made the sea disappear? Who called it back in again?'

'What do you mean, *who*?'

'Was it you, Fortune?'

'Of course it wasn't!' I cried. 'The sea isn't like a dog! You can't bid it to come and go at will!'

'Did you cast a spell on Susannah Spicer's needlework, then?'

'No! I've told you, I'm not a witch!'

Mr Hopkins put his pen aside and folded his arms. 'Yet the evidence is stacked against you. If only Mr Spicer were still here to clear your name. But he perished that day, didn't he? Dr Blood tells me you weren't overly fond of the man.'

I didn't speak.

'Well?' he asked.

I ground my teeth in frustration.

'Come now,' Mr Hopkins said, impatience creeping into his tone. 'Has the devil stolen your tongue?'

Still, I didn't answer: he'd only twist my words if I did.

'Very well. We'll try something else.' He snapped his fingers at the soldiers. 'Search her for moles, birthmarks, anything unusual. A witch will bear the marks of her kind.'

I shrank back in my seat. The soldiers grabbed my arms, pushing up my sleeves. When they didn't find what they were looking for, they yanked off my cap, pulling at my hair, checking behind my ears. I ducked away, which made them rougher.

It was only when I finally started crying that they stopped – and hastily too, jumping away from me as if I was poxed.

'Don't ever touch a witch's tears!' Fierce Soldier warned. 'She'll use them to curse us!'

'Isn't it that witches *don't* cry?' the other soldier asked.

They both looked at me, suddenly not sure *what* I was.

Mr Hopkins dropped to his knees, seizing my feet before I'd the wit to kick him.

'Look harder, friends,' he said, almost gleeful. 'See this mark here on her left foot?'

I tried to wriggle free, but he held me impossibly tight.

'It's a birthmark, that's all!' I stammered. The mark was only small, about the size of an acorn and as unremarkable. It'd been there all my life.

Yet you'd have thought Mr Hopkins had found manna from heaven. From his pocket, he produced an implement that might've been for opening wine flagons or coring a cheese, except it ended in a needle – a hefty one too. The sight of it made me tremble.

'This,' he explained, to the soldiers rather than me, 'is my witch tester. I'm going to put it to use.'

28

I hoped beyond hope that he was jesting, or very poorly in the mind. Yet looming over me with a needle big enough for knitting wool, Mr Hopkins looked dangerously sane. He was still holding my foot in his free hand: no amount of squirming would make him release it. I twisted as far as I could away from him, which wasn't far enough by a mile.

'I don't much care for needles,' I tried to reason.

He spoke only to the soldiers. 'If she's a witch the needle will go in without pain. And you'll witness no injury—'

He jabbed at my foot.

The shock made me jump. So did the fact it didn't hurt, though not for the reasons he claimed.

'It's a trick!' I blurted out. 'The needle clicked. It retracted! I heard it!'

'I did too,' the quieter soldier admitted. Fierce Soldier breathed in sharply.

Mr Hopkins removed his device, beckoning the soldiers forward to inspect my foot. I gritted my teeth, hating them all.

'There's no wound on the skin!' Fierce Soldier said in disbelief.

Mr Hopkins nodded calmly. 'As I expected. The needle has no effect on her. Because she is a witch.'

'It didn't go in!' I protested.

But the soldiers were now edging towards the door.

'Where are you going?' Mr Hopkins asked, surprised.

Fierce Soldier spread his hands. 'Master Hopkins, this here is a *child* and what you're doing to her, well, it's not right.'

'Indeed, it's torture,' the quieter one muttered.

I felt unexpectedly hopeful again. Was this it, then? Was it over?

'Torture? Gentlemen, I've barely started,' Mr Hopkins said coolly.

'We'll find you someone else to guard her,' Fierce Soldier replied.

They couldn't get out of the door fast enough. Mr Hopkins hurried after them, though not before securing me to the stool, and taking all but one of the candles with him.

I sat there in the almost-dark, thinking *now what?*

Was someone coming back? Were they going to just leave me here?

I wasn't going to wait and find out.

Mr Hopkins, the brute, had tied my wrists to the legs of the stool. Thinking I might manage to undo the knots with my teeth, I leaned forward. It wasn't easy to keep my balance, and just as I'd got my head between my knees, the key rasped in the lock and the door opened again.

Upside down I saw a person enter, wearing worn, muddy shoes. The stool tipped. Chin first, I went sprawling to the floor. The force of the blow made me bite my own cheek. I tasted blood. The new guard heaved me off the floor. As the room righted itself again, I saw he was wearing a cloak, the hood of which was raised. He didn't look like the soldiers. He was younger, thin about the shoulders.

'I've been given orders to keep you walking – all day and night if I have to,' the guard said in a very gruff voice.

Something about him annoyed me. Maybe it was because I sensed he was only a little older than me. He also sounded as if he had a very sore throat – either that or he was trying a bit too hard to act older than his years.

'What for?' I snapped.

'Imps,' the guard replied.

I stared at him. '*Imps*? The little green creatures?'

'Mr Hopkins says if a witch is exhausted, that's when she's most likely to be taken over by evil spirits to do their bidding,' the guard explained. 'And those spirits often take the form of imps.'

'Then Mr Hopkins is a complete cod-brain,' I muttered under my breath.

The guard tried not to smile.

'I'm to keep you walking, miss,' he said. 'Even when you're fit to drop.'

'Do what you will, then.' I was weary enough already. I'd no idea fear could be so exhausting – and anger, and frustration – all eating away at me because it was obvious they weren't going to let me go.

Once he'd untied my wrists from the stool, the guard started walking me up and down, up and down. It wasn't a big room – seven paces either way, at the most. We were turning so often I soon felt dizzy. I hated Mr Hopkins. I hated Dr Blood and his greedy plans to win favour with the king. I wasn't overly fond of this new guard, either, who was following his instructions to the letter.

When a bang on the door came, and a call of 'Open up!' I felt another stupid rush of hope. Mr Hopkins didn't come inside. He merely handed over another candle and told the guard he'd be back at dawn.

'I'm counting on you, boy,' Mr Hopkins said. 'I should've trusted a local guard all along.'

The door closed. The key ground in the lock. Outside in the passageway, Mr Hopkins' footfalls faded to silence. The thought of being here all night made me so despairing, I barely noticed the guard taking my arm and gently guiding me back to sit on the stool. Only when he said, 'I'm going to untie you now,' did I look up.

The voice, no longer gruff, was Jem's. So was the face peering at me, which I could see now he'd dropped the hood of his cloak. I shut my eyes and opened them again, just in case it was a trick of the light. But there was no mistaking Jem's narrow face and kind grey eyes.

'Brother!' I gasped. 'What are you doing here?'

'I could ask you the same,' he replied.

For the briefest moment, I wondered if he was still angry with me. But I was so overwhelmingly glad to see him, I started to cry in earnest.

'Oh, Jem,' I sobbed. 'Things have taken a very sorry turn, haven't they?'

'Indeed they have,' he agreed, and there were tears in his eyes too, which he quickly sniffed away. 'But shush now, hold still or I'll never get these knots undone.'

The second he'd untied me, I flung my arms around him. He smelled so familiar – of sea salt and sackcloth – it made me cry all the more.

'I've missed you,' I snivelled into his shoulder.

'Let's never fight again.' He staggered a little under my weight. 'Whoa, you've got bigger these past months!'

'You've got saucier,' I replied, tweaking his ear. 'Last time I saw you, you were the blessed child of Fair Maidens Lane. What happened? Why are you working here?'

He ducked away, suddenly serious. 'Remember that night Mother took you from your bed?'

'Insisting it was time I found work? That I'd do better as a boy?' Oh, I remembered it, all right.

'She was terrified they'd come for you next. That's why she did it.'

I groaned, head in hands. We should never have gone out in our boat on the Sabbath. My inkling about Mother had been right all along: she'd lied about the need for me to earn money. She'd sent me to the hiring fair hoping I'd be safer away from Fair Maidens Lane.

'The flood has made things ten times worse,' Jem went on. 'It's like fever, this fear of witchcraft – it's not just the landowners using it as an excuse to get their hands on our land. Everyone's got a dose of it. And now the king's coming to Somerset, and we all know his thoughts on witches. It's hardly going to calm things down.'

I looked up. 'You haven't told me yet why you're working here.'

'They needed local guards. How I saw it, if I was on duty when they brought you in, well, I might be to able help you. I'm sorry, I couldn't think what else to do.'

'Wait ... You *knew* I was going to be arrested?'

He gave a half nod. 'These past few days the rumours started again. Everyone's saying the same thing, that witches are to blame, and the suspects should be arrested. Your name kept being mentioned.'

'Why me?'

'Because, dear sister, you've always been a bit *different*. And once we'd been seen out in the sea on the Sabbath, well, it didn't take long for people to seize on a name ...'

'That Dr Blood is an evil piece,' I said, slumping back in my seat. 'You know he's been spying on our hamlet right from the start? At least, the man he hired has.'

'That's not the worst of it, either,' Jem replied miserably. 'Oh, Fortune, they're taking you to the Assizes. A proper witch trial, it'll be, laid on for the king's benefit.'

Fear twisted in my chest. But I fought it because there was a way out of this. It would take courage, and a fair bit of running – all the way down the coast to where the *Songbird* was about to set sail.

'Jem,' I said, trying to be calm. 'That key you've got. How many doors does it open?'

'All of them. Now do you see why I work here?'

Absolutely I did.

'Have you heard of a place called Withy Cove?' I asked.

'I have. It's a few miles east of town. Why?'

'That's where we need to go. There are people I know – people who can help us. I can't go back home, not yet, and neither can you once it's known you've freed me.'

'Can't we do this on our own, just us?'

'We need them, Jem. They've got a boat, and they'll take us far away from here.'

His smile was affectionate and sad. 'I once said I'd never get in a boat with you again, don't you remember?'

I did. But, oh my word, how times had changed.

29

After declaring no one was out in the passageway, Jem unlocked the door. He went first, hand cupped around a candle flame, wearing my wool jacket. I followed in the disguise of his cloak.

'Witch marks,' Jem said, pointing out fresh scratches on the beams in the wall. They looked like letters, a jumble of 'v's and 'm's overlapping each other. 'They're all through the town hall, to protect people from—'

'Me,' I realised grimly.

Jem winced. 'Sorry, sister. You need to know what you're facing, and be ready.'

But as we headed down the passage, I wasn't ready at all. I was trembling. And it grew worse as we climbed the steps to the ground floor, and heard the roar of the crowd outside.

'H-how m-many people are out there, exactly?' I stuttered.

'A fair few,' Jem admitted.

We came out into an empty hallway. There were tapestries on one wall, a coat of arms on the other, and a black and white chequered floor that stretched all the way to where Jem was pointing. 'That's the back door. Your way out. Keep your head down, and when it's safe to run, run.'

I was struggling to think straight. Just as long as we got to Withy Cove, that was what mattered.

'What about you? What will you do?' I asked.

'I'll slip out after you. I'll find Miss Spicer and tell her what's happening. Wait for me out on the Bridgwater road. Make sure your face is covered.'

I checked my hood. My hands were shaking.

Something caught Jem's attention. As he put a finger to his lips, I heard the approaching footsteps. He waved me away, pointing at the door again and mouthing 'Go!' Then, lifting the corner of the tapestry, he slid behind it: it covered all but the tips of his toes.

I was alone – or as good as – only for a moment before two men swaggered into view. They had the well-fed, well-clad appearance of landowners, our unfriendly neighbours perhaps: I didn't look too closely. I was more concerned that they'd spotted me. And they had, though only in the same way you see a chair or cupboard so as not to walk into it. They swept past and were gone.

I breathed again, checked my hood one final time, and made for the door. The noise outside seemed to press against the walls, the windows.

Don't listen, I told myself. Keep your head down and walk.

The back door flew open so fast I wasn't ready. The noise of the crowd hit me like a punch.

'Get rid of the little witch!'

'We don't want her sort round here!'

'I never trusted the look of her – one day a girl, next day a boy.'

'I heard she cursed her poor father, that's why he drowned.'

Go! Jem's voice said inside my head.

I took a couple of steps. Stopped. Between the building and the edge of the crowd salt had been sprinkled in a line on the ground. It was an age-old custom to ward off evil: everyone knew no true witch would dare cross salt.

'Walk over it, then, lad, and be on your way,' said a rosy-cheeked woman who'd stopped yelling long enough to see me hesitate.

The fact she'd thought me a guard spurred me on. Don't jinx it, I told myself. You're not free yet.

The crowd was ten, maybe fifteen bodies deep. I

skirted the outer edge, keeping to the gutter. It was hard to believe that these were normal Somerset people, not monsters: women in plain frocks and bonnets with babies on their hips, men flushed with cider, children eating hot chestnuts or picking their noses or both.

In amongst the crush, I spotted a tall, serious woman with yellow plaited hair. And with her, a girl in a bonnet, two similar plaits poking out underneath. Both were on tiptoe, anxiously craning their necks to see what was happening. Standing beside Abigail, small and frightened-looking, was another girl in breeches, trying to shush a crying baby.

How I wanted to call their names and rush over and wrap my arms round them and tell them that they should leave Somerset with me and come to Withy Cove. It was agony to keep walking, leaving all that to Jem.

Away from the very front, the noise quickly dropped to that of normal market-day chatter. It wasn't so hard, then, to believe I'd stepped back into my old life, and these were just people gossiping on the roadside as they'd always done. The crowd thinned. Under my feet, the cobbles turned to dirt. And I was out the other side. The road that would take me to Withy Cove lay before me. I'd almost made it.

''Tis only another lad coming out,' I heard someone mutter.

A quick glance behind confirmed Jem was now following. I could see the grey of my jacket weaving through the crowd towards where Mother and Susannah were standing.

'Then who in heaven's name *is* inside still?' another woman replied.

A fresh wave of angry noise spread through the crowd. People began moving towards the town hall, looking for all the world as if they were going to storm the building. I turned to run. Turned back again to check Jem was still coming, and there he was, fighting through the mass like a swimmer.

'Keep walking!' he mouthed to me. 'Go!'

As I tried to, someone grabbed me by the shoulder.

'Not so fast, Fortune Sharpe.' I glimpsed a pair of salt-white cuffs.

It was Mr Hopkins, two new thuggish guards flanking him.

I was caught.

Twisting my arms behind my back, the guards pushed me towards a waiting carriage.

'We're going on a little journey, you and I,' Mr

Hopkins said. 'To somewhere I know you'll be more comfortable.'

And oh how nicely he put it, as if he was taking me to the king's own palace.

30

Ilchester gaol was a terrible place, full of noises and smells that were barely human. In my cell alone, there were six other women. The two who were conscious introduced themselves as Mad Meg and Twelve-toed Tess, and demanded to know what grisly crime I'd committed.

'Apparently, I bewitched the sea,' I said.

'Is that *all*?' Mad Meg looked disappointed.

Twelve-toed Tess cackled. 'Welcome to our home, Little Miss Neptune.'

The name stuck, as did the pair of them to me. They didn't stop talking all night, though the other four women stayed slumped against the wall, even when rats nosed through their hair.

*

On the morning of the Assizes I woke wavering between hope and despair. I was cold, sore, aching with hunger.

No one was going to rescue me. Jem had probably been caught by now, and the *Songbird* would've set sail hours ago, so what did it matter if the world thought I was a witch and punished me according to the law? Though I still couldn't quite believe they'd find me guilty of something so ridiculous, so totally *untrue,* and it was this I was clinging on to by my fingertips.

'Rather you than me,' said Mad Meg, whose crime had been to dig up her neighbour's cabbages. 'I've heard Mr Hopkins is a brute.'

'Slippery as an eel,' agreed Twelve-toed Tess. She'd been fined for chasing her sister with a horsewhip, but couldn't pay so was in prison.

As they chatted on over my head, I sat hugging my knees until the guard arrived. He was as tall as he was wide, with a neck like a fat, pink ham.

'Well, Sharpe, we've got a journey to Glastonbury ahead of us,' he said briskly. 'I trust you're ready.'

My heart sank. Glastonbury: so I *was* returning there, despite my insistence to Susannah that I never would.

The guard, impatient, rattled the cell bars with his baton. 'On your feet, then! Let's be having you!

'Keep it down, Mr Nelson,' Mad Meg complained. 'Or you'll have our nerves in tatters.'

'Bit late to worry about that,' he replied. 'The king's already in Somerset. He's come to witness Sharpe's trial.'

My cell mates squealed.

'King James? The Scot?' Mad Meg gave her filthy hair a pat.

Twelve-toed Tess rounded on me. 'Kept that to yourself, didn't you, girlie?'

It wasn't that I'd forgotten – more that I'd blocked it from my mind. To be reminded of it now, when things were grim enough, made me feel properly ill.

'Well, well, Little Miss Neptune, what a dark horse you are,' Twelve-toed Tess murmured.

'Boys' clothes, a boy's haircut, the dirtiest face you ever saw,' Mr Nelson mused. 'You only need to look at her to see the guilt.' Though when he unlocked the cell, Mad Meg jammed her foot against the door so he couldn't open it.

'You're right,' she told him. 'She can't go to trial looking like that.'

'Rules are rules, Meg,' the guard warned. 'I can't keep the King of the British Isles waiting.'

Twelve-toed Tess moved closer to the bars. She was intimidatingly tall.

'And there's me thinking you'd be on the side of the

underdog, Mr Nelson.' She tutted. 'Dear me, our royal visitor seems to have turned your head.'

'At least give the kid a fighting chance,' Mad Meg pleaded.

I expected him to barge in and take me, yet begrudgingly he gave us five more minutes. He even brought a pail of water and someone's old gown for me to wear.

'We're going to sort you out,' Mad Meg informed me. 'Sometimes, even if you don't feel like it on the inside, it's best to look the part.'

Before I could argue, Twelve-toed Tess pushed me to the ground and sat on my legs. In a whirl of cloth they scrubbed my face, my hands, my feet. Mad Meg used her fingers to unknot my hair and plait it – at least that's what she said she was doing. I was sure she was scalping me alive. The dress was huge, but once its sleeves were turned up and its waist tied with string, I did look more presentable.

'Thank you.' My voice wobbled; I couldn't help crying when they'd been kind to me.

Mad Meg pinched my cheek.

'Go well, Little Miss Neptune,' said Twelve-toed Tess.

The cell door opened. Irons were clamped on

my wrists. Mr Nelson led me away, and as I glanced behind, they blew me a kiss.

*

The next faces I saw were considerably less friendly. Approaching Glastonbury we had our first view of the crowds. At this distance they were little more than ant-like specks covering the hillside and running along the edge of the floodwater. As we got closer the specks became people-shaped, with hats, bonnets, shawls, collars, and eyes that eagerly followed the cart's progress to the foot of the hill. There were hundreds here, possibly more.

I clung to the side of the cart, shivering. It was best not to look. Best to keep my head down and remember to breathe. But I was desperate for a glimpse of my family or Susannah, and so for better or worse, scanned the crowds.

'Brought the pamphleteers flocking, you have.' Mr Nelson pointed out a group of men in smart town clothes, who were already writing things down. 'They'll be reading all about you in London by tomorrow.'

I gulped. 'So soon?'

The thought of strangers hearing my pack-of-lies

story made me long for Jem or Mother or Susannah even more. But I couldn't find them in the sea of people. Everything had become a blur of hostile faces. I didn't trust myself to focus on anyone again until the cart came to a halt at the very front of the crowds.

Someone had brought out a parlour table and set it on the grass. Behind it, on straight-backed chairs, sat three gentlemen. Two of these men I knew all too well – Dr Blood in black, with his plump beetle body, and Mr Hopkins, who kept his scar turned away from the crowd. I felt bile creeping up my throat: how I hated them both.

The third man was rather small, with a sandy-coloured beard. To be honest, but for the huge froth of lace at his collar he looked quite ordinary, though my cell mates' eyes, I bet, would've stood out of their heads. And even I, in my wretched state, had to stare. For this was King James of the British Isles, the greatest witch hunter of them all.

'Bring the prisoner forward for her test,' Dr Blood instructed.

'Test? What test?' I asked as Mr Nelson handed me down from the cart.

Knowingly, he tapped the side of his nose. 'Let's just say you'll be having another wash very soon.'

I'd no idea what he meant, or why my wrist irons were now being unlocked, only to be replaced with rope, which was looped around my waist. More guards surrounded me.

I was bewildered. Why wasn't anyone asking me questions? Wouldn't I at least get a chance to speak?

Someone was tugging at the rope around my waist. A sudden jolt and I was dragged backwards across the grass towards the water till I was in it up to my ankles.

'What are you doing?' I cried.

'Quieten her!' said a stern voice. On his feet, and holding another coil of rope, was Mr Hopkins.

'Sir, what's happening?' I begged. 'You said I was to be put to trial at the Assizes. Why am I in the water?'

'Tie her,' Mr Hopkins instructed the guards.

Someone grabbed my right arm. Another guard wound rope round my hand. It all happened so fast – the pushing, pulling, pinching. And then the same guard grabbed my left foot.

'Let go of me!' I shrieked.

He was far stronger than me, and yanked my foot so hard I lost my balance and fell. I hit the shallow water with an almighty smack. In panic, I tried to get up again, but there were guards all around me. My mouth was full of mud. Someone was pulling me again, forcing my upper body down towards my feet.

I fought hard. I screamed. Yet in a moment it was done. The guards stood back, breathless, admiring their work. Like a lamb going to market, they'd bound me, hand to foot, right to left. I prayed my family and Susannah weren't here, after all. I couldn't bear for them to see me like this.

A bell rang to quieten the crowd, before Mr Hopkins addressed them.

'Fortune Sharpe will be tested today in the very floods she is accused of luring here from the coast.'

I lay on my side in the water, terrified.

'We must protect our souls from the threat of dark magic that is infecting our people,' he went on.

A savage cheer went up from the crowd. Just like yesterday in Bridgwater, they were hungry for revenge or justice, or I didn't know what, their noise a confusing rumble in my head.

Why me? What had I done to make them hate me so much? I was a plain, ordinary child from a hamlet by the sea. These people didn't know one true thing about who I was.

'The accused will be ducked under the water,' Mr Hopkins explained. His voice was calm and clear. 'If

238

she sinks and drowns, she is innocent. But if she floats, then that is proof of her being a witch, a crime which is punishable by death.'

The guards moved in. One pulled the rope. Another seized my shoulders. They pulled me away from the edge, away from Mr Hopkins. The water grew colder and deeper. The ground beneath me fell away. The guards were holding me up so I was bobbing, floating.

Above me the sky was softest grey. Water lapped around my head, my ears, over my face. I let my fear go: I had no use for it any more. Instead, I pictured Bea's pink-gummed smile, and wondered whether the *Songbird* had yet hit the open seas. And if what Maira told me about the caul could really, possibly, be true.

The guards pushed me under.

31

Beneath the water I couldn't hear the crowd. It was almost peaceful. No more shouting, no more chanting of 'Witch! Witch! Witch!' The cold was brutal, squeezing my head, pressing my lungs. Yet I felt overwhelmingly calm, as if the water was protecting me, somehow, and down here I was safe.

Dark spots flickered before my eyes. My mind, like it did right on the edge of sleep, began to drift away. This, I supposed, was drowning. All that fuss about the caul had been for nothing, because no amount of good luck was going to save me now.

And yet, with a jolt, I was suddenly alert. The dark spots were mud. Something was moving through the water. Everything turned cloudy as a pair of feet kicked their way towards me. It couldn't be Jem because he was a weak swimmer. But I didn't know anyone else with such long spindly legs, such grubby breeches.

Two arms hooked themselves under my armpits, and

I was lifted up towards the light. We broke the surface together, coughing and heaving for breath.

'Hold still,' Jem spluttered as he worked free the knot binding my right thumb to my left toe.

Once I was no longer bent double, I could float. And then it was me helping Jem, who was shaking like fury.

'Lord, how I hate deep water,' he gasped.

I couldn't believe he'd got past the guards, let alone swum in to rescue me.

'But you're here!' I cried. 'You saved me!' And he'd be joking about it for years to come if we got out of here alive.

'You're n-nnot saved y-yyyet, not with them there,' Jem stuttered through chattering teeth.

He meant the crowd. The chanting had turned to yelling. I couldn't tell what the words were, only that they sounded ready to rip us to shreds. What's more, they'd come closer, spilling down the hillside to stand right at the water's edge. They were spread all along it, arms linked in a menacing wall.

We had to do something – and fast – because if the crowd didn't finish us off, then this freezing water would. Even behind us, the rowing boat was still approaching. We were surrounded. Jem looked as terrified as I was. Our only choice – and it wasn't really one at all – was to face our accusers.

'We'll stick together,' I decided. 'Two of us will be harder to deal with.'

We swam slowly, knowing every stroke brought us closer to the shore. About twenty yards out, the guards waded in to meet us. There were four of them. Two seized me, the other two took Jem. They were rough, clearly expecting a struggle, though we'd barely strength to stand.

At the front of the crowd was Dr Blood.

'Take them both to stand before the king! At once!' he roared.

The crowd parted sullenly. We were hauled across to the table where King James was seated. Mr Hopkins was already on his feet.

'How DARE you interrupt justice!' His voice was hushed and deadlier for it. He glared over the top of my head at Jem. 'YOU, boy, shall be punished for this.'

'Sir,' Jem spoke with all the dignity he could muster. 'I only did what any brother would. My sister is innocent of all charges.'

In that moment, I loved Jem so much it hurt. Yet his words slid over the men like butter in a hot pan.

'I get results, Master Sharpe, that's what people pay

me for,' Mr Hopkins replied coldly. 'Your sister didn't drown, therefore she *is* guilty as charged.'

'And thou shalt not suffer a witch to live,' Dr Blood added.

I knew the line, all right. It was from the new King James Bible, and the way Dr Blood glanced at the king – fawning, desperate – wasn't a good sign. We'd made him look bad in front of royalty. He wasn't about to forget it, either.

'You're not . . . I mean, you can't . . .' I protested.

Jem kept on trying to reason. 'Gentlemen, I beg you, Fortune might be a bit of an oddity with her short hair and boys' garments, but she's no witch.'

'Get the boy out of my sight,' Mr Hopkins snarled.

Dr Blood twisted round to beckon more guards. But they were distracted by someone jostling at the front of the crowd.

'Take your hands off me!' the woman cried. 'I can stand by myself. I don't need assistance.'

I blinked. It couldn't be.

Maira was supposed to be miles away at sea. Yet it was her, no question, standing a head taller than the guards, and quicker too, sidestepping them with ease. Shoulders back, chin raised, she marched straight up to the king's table.

'Those friends at Withy Cove I told you about?' I muttered to Jem. 'She's the boat's captain.'

'I know,' Jem muttered back. 'I fetched her.'

A rush of pride came over me – at my brother, and at Maira, who was standing before the three men, arms folded, feet apart.

'What interruption can we possibly have *now*?' Mr Hopkins was beginning to lose his cool. 'Resolve it, Blood, for heaven's sake!'

Dr Blood took his frustration out on the guards. 'What are you waiting for? Get rid of this ... this ... *woman*! And the boy! They're interrupting justice—'

'Justice? Pah!' Maira spat at his feet.

For the first time King James looked mildly interested. 'Pray, who is this disorderly wench?'

'A friend of the accused, clearly,' Mr Hopkins replied. 'And therefore a witch by association.'

A look passed between him and Dr Blood. A nod. An agreement. They both turned to me, hard-eyed as ever. I felt my legs go weak. The guards who were holding me tightened their grip.

'What the ... ?' I realised what was happening. Me *and* Maira? They couldn't accuse *both* of us.

More guards started closing in on Maira. Again,

she sidestepped them, to jab a finger at Dr Blood. '*He* knows who I am.'

I couldn't imagine how. Yet they clearly had met before, their dislike for each other very obvious.

'The woman is mistaken.' Dr Blood tried to brush it off. 'She's in league with Fortune Sharpe. We do not need to hear any more from either of them.'

After all, who were we but two worthless females, whereas he was a man with status. He had wealth and a voice. Well, he'd seriously underestimated Maira.

'Oh, I'm mistaken, am I?' She raised an eyebrow – and what power there was in that look. 'You don't even *know* the person *you* and your business partner hired to bring your sugar cargo to this country? I'd say that was careless, wouldn't you?'

Sugar.

The white devil, Mistress Bagwell used to call it. It made people rich and tasted like heaven on a plate, yet what it did to teeth and morals left a lot to be desired. So even Maira was part of the trade that bound Dr Blood and Mr Spicer together. I didn't know what I'd expected her ship to carry, but it hadn't occurred to me it might be sugar.

I remembered then what Mr Spicer had said on

Twelfth Night, about the captain with too many opinions who'd refused to take a certain cargo.

Maira.

It all tied in with her disappearance at the hiring fair. Susannah was probably right: something had spooked her, and that something, for whatever reason, was Mr Spicer.

'Yes, that's why I'm here, gentlemen,' Maira said, still unbelievably calm. 'To tell you the true nature of this trial, which has nothing to do with witchcraft, and everything to do with the sugar trade.'

The men looked unconvinced by this, which spurred me on to speak up. It was now or never.

'What she says is true,' I insisted. 'I too once worked for Mr Thomas Spicer, of Berrow Hall, Somersetshire.'

'Indeed, where you lied as to your sex, and were employed as a *male* servant to Mr Spicer's son,' Dr Blood retorted, recovering his stride.

The crowd tittered. King James rolled his eyes. He was starting to look bored.

'And so we have on trial, a liar and a ship's captain who goes back on her word. Hardly two of our most upstanding citizens, are they?' Dr Blood said, so smugly I had to grit my teeth.

Maira didn't flinch. 'Mr Spicer – and Dr

Blood – wanted my ship and crew to carry a different type of cargo across the Atlantic. We refused.'

'Really, I hardly think—' Mr Hopkins tried to interrupt, but the king silenced him with a glare.

'To keep up with the world's demand for sugar, huge plantations are needed, worked by huge numbers of people. White men – very rich white men – are taking men, women and children from Africa,' Maira continued. 'From the jungle, to work their crops like animals. If you're dark of skin you're not human, that's how they see it.'

Whether the king agreed with her or not, I couldn't tell, but he was listening. So was the entire crowd.

'Mr Spicer and Dr Blood,' Maira went on. 'They no longer wanted just sugar to be shipped. They asked me to sail by West Africa and pick up a very different type of cargo; one that's living. Slaves.'

I knew in my gut that this wasn't good. The hiring fair had been grim enough with its prodding and poking; this was a hundred times worse. I glanced at Jem, who looked as horrified as I was.

'And you said no?' the king asked Maira.

'I did.'

The king sat back in his seat as he thought over what Maira had said. We watched. Waited. You could feel the whole crowd holding their breath.

Yet when he did speak, it was almost a whine. 'Please don't tell me I've come all this way to hear an argument about sugar.'

'It's not just about sugar.' Maira raised her voice. 'It's because I was a woman saying no!'

'And you're also a witch,' Dr Blood reminded her.

'Ah yes, the witch trial,' King James interrupted. 'Shall we resume proceedings?'

A roar went up. Someone shouted, 'Witch!' The chanting began all over again.

32

New ropes appeared. The guards on either side of me tied my arms. More men were brought in to do the same to Maira, who fought with all her might until she was overwhelmed. The moment had turned with bewildering speed.

'Drown the witches!'

'Cast them out!'

'Witch! Witch! Witch!'

The guards dragged us back to the floodwater. Somewhere in the confusion was Jem, fighting to stay with me, trying to pull me back.

'Stop! You can't duck me again!' I screamed at the guards.

'This isn't justice!' Maira yelled.

At the water's edge, Dr Blood, who was leading the way, came to a sudden stop.

'You cannot come ashore here!' he cried.

Something was wrong. There were raised voices.

Gesturing arms. The fuss seemed to be about the little rowing boat that had just pulled in to the shallows, and the group climbing ashore from its prow. Under arms, between shoulders, I glimpsed curly brown hair, a baby in a sling, two sets of yellow plaits.

A huge wave of love came over me. Then total, absolute panic that my family and Susannah had walked straight into this dreadful situation. It was Susannah's well-bred voice that carried above the crowd.

'If you truly believe that magic controls the sea,' she was saying, 'then I'm the one you should be blaming, not Fortune Sharpe or Maira.'

'Stop your mouth!' I cried to her. 'Go, quickly! Be safe!'

The crowd shrank back, a space opening around the new arrivals. Susannah was standing on the grass, very small, very composed. Bea was in her arms, rubbing her eyes as if she'd just woken up. Mother and Abigail were behind them, leaving the water.

Mr Hopkins elbowed his way through, muttering about charging extra for his time if things didn't hurry up. But suddenly all of us were herded back towards the king. I felt weak with relief, though all this stopping and starting was doing nothing to steady my nerves.

'If this is a proper trial, then the defendants must be

allowed to speak,' Mother declared in the same tone she used when handling difficult cows.

Mr Hopkins shook his head.

It was the king himself who seemed to agree with her. 'Indeed, it has been most unsatisfactory so far. And who are you?'

Mother raised her gaze to look at him directly. 'Mistress Sharpe. Fortune is my daughter and she's no witch.'

I should have been surprised at her courage, but I wasn't. Mother had chased after Old Margaret's cart with a milking stool, so she wasn't going to let her own daughter be drowned without putting up a fight. Standing there, fierce-faced, she looked like a Viking warrior. Abigail was a smaller version of the same. I tried not to sob with gratitude.

'And you are?' The king's beringed finger pointed at Susannah. Bea, spotting the glinting emerald on it, reached out with glee.

'Susannah Spicer, Your Majesty,' she replied.

'Spicer, hmmm ...'

'Daughter of my business partner,' Dr Blood informed him.

The king wafted his hand vaguely. 'No, no ... that's not who I was thinking of.'

There was muttering. More dagger-sharp glances passing between Dr Blood and Mr Hopkins. I was confused and exhausted and wanting this all to be over. Beside me, Maira let out a huge, fed-up groan.

'Look, I've got a ship to sail. Business to do. So perhaps someone can explain to me why that makes me a witch. What exactly *is* this all about?' she asked.

It was me who answered.

'It's about fear,' I said, surprising myself rather.

The king's eyebrows shot up. '*Fear?*'

Now I'd started, I kept going. 'There are things, like the sea, that we can't control. So if we try to blame someone for it, it makes us less scared. And it seems to me that we always pick on the weak ones, the strange ones, the ones who aren't like us.'

I glanced at Susannah and Jem, at Mother and Abigail. We'd talked about these things between us, in private. We all knew what it felt like to be the person who was singled out.

'The wave that struck our coast?' I hurried on. 'You could blame it on magic or witchcraft. It helps to have a reason, because then you can try to stop it happening again.'

'I've heard enough of this drivel,' Dr Blood insisted. 'Guards! Resume the trial!'

And I'd had enough of this nasty little man, of being cold and terrified. My temper was on the rise.

'Mr Spicer's son told me all about your business dealings, and what you were after,' I said to him.

'You *dared* to speak of my business to Master Spicer?' Dr Blood was stunned. 'As if it were any concern of yours?'

'Oh, but it is, sir,' I insisted. 'My life may be of little value to you, but it is to me. Because of your *plans* I'm on trial for something I'm innocent of.'

'Wait,' the king interrupted. 'What plans?'

I answered first: 'Your navy, Your Majesty. Mr Spicer and Dr Blood wanted your protection – that's what Ellis told me. They knew their cargo was risky. In truth, they probably knew it was wrong. But they needed your naval ships to protect them from attack.'

'She's lying,' Dr Blood cut in. 'Yet again.'

'This whole witch trial, Your Majesty,' I spoke over him, 'is their way of impressing you and getting you to support their business. It's never been about evil.'

'Seize her! Take her to the flood again! Take both of these witches!' Dr Blood cried.

I braced myself for the soldiers' crushing grip on my arms. But they didn't move. No one was looking at us any more. They were nudging each other, pointing at Dr Blood.

'Ellis, you say? Ellis Spicer?' the king asked, sitting forward in his seat. '*The* Ellis Spicer?'

It threw me completely. I looked to Susannah, who was hanging on the king's every word.

'Ummm ... yes,' I said, without thinking. 'The acrobat.'

The king's face changed. For one fear-filled moment, I was sure I'd said a terrible thing, and not only was my own fate sealed but Ellis's too, wherever he might be. But the king slapped his knees heartily and laughed out loud.

'Ha! Ellis Spicer! Would you believe such a thing?' he cried.

'No, Your Majesty,' I replied, not having a clue what he meant. I glanced at Susannah, who shrugged helplessly.

'Do you know that I met this very fellow just a couple of days ago? He entertained me, he and his troupe, on the evening we broke our travel. And what a marvellous performance it was.'

I stared at the king. 'You saw him? Alive? Ellis Spicer?'

'Of course. The young man introduced himself by name. I've plans to invite him to the palace for our Easter festivities.'

'Oh, thank goodness!' I gasped. 'This is very fine news indeed.' Susannah burst into tears.

I was thrilled that Ellis was alive, truly I was. I wasn't sure if it was enough to save Maira and me, though there was no denying that the mood had changed again.

The king was now eyeing Dr Blood with disdain.

'If what the child says is true then you have duped me, Blood,' he said. 'You have enticed me here to Somerset, not to see justice being done, but to further your own ends.'

'You cannot believe her,' Dr Blood insisted, very flustered. 'The girl is evil.'

'The only evil I've seen here in Somerset has come from witch hunters,' I retorted.

Now it was Mr Hopkins who turned on Dr Blood.

'I took on this case in good faith,' he said, shaking his head. 'I shall send my bill directly. Now if someone could bring me my horse, I'll be on my way.'

'But Mr Hopkins, Your Majesty—' Dr Blood spluttered.

'Enough of this. You're a good dentist, Blood, but a terrible businessman. Think again on your cargo. Exploration is my new investment. I've sent that Raleigh fellow to South America in search of gold. You'd be wise invest in something similar.'

Dr Blood dropped his head in defeat. 'Yes, Your Majesty.'

'And for heaven's sake leave the Spicer family and their acquaintances ALONE!'

*

So it was, like a deck of cards, the trial fell to pieces. And I, for the second time, was saved. It wasn't all over though, until King James had absolved me of guilt. I was made to stand in front of him, looking suitably meek. It wasn't hard to do, either, when I trembled from head to foot with cold. Susannah was struggling to hold Bea, who wanted to get to Jem, get to Mother's plaits, get to the king's buckled shoes.

The very second my innocence was declared, Bea lunged for the king's hand. She'd seen his giant emerald ring and wanted to grab it.

'I'm sorry.' Susannah blushed, trying to pull her away. 'But you saw my brother – where?'

'In a town somewhere miles from here,' the king said, vague again. 'Dorset? Devon, maybe?'

Susannah tried to press him but he didn't seem to remember, or perhaps he was too taken with Bea.

'So this little cherub is Ellis Spicer's sister, eh?' He chucked her under the chin. 'Do you know what a funny, brilliant entertainer your brother is, do you?'

'EEEwwwooo,' Bea replied.

Meanwhile, I was dying to ask what had happened to Susannah's crewel-work piece, since no one had mentioned it at the trial. I waited until the fuss had died down. 'Your Majesty, what did you think of the crewel work Dr Blood showed you?'

'Mistress Spicer's design?'

I nodded.

'Well, she has a talent, that can't be denied. The queen will admire it greatly, though it wasn't really to my taste.'

'You didn't *like* it?'

'I prefer a scene or a picture I can recognise. This piece was rather too elaborate and certainly didn't prove anything, not to my eyes.'

So the king had looked at the piece and seen only patterns: not an enormous wave or a boy with a yellow feather in his cap running away from the sea. He'd seen what he wanted to see, and passed judgement. How familiar that sounded! If I never saw a needle and thread ever again, I decided, it would still be far too soon.

*

When his carriage was finally summoned, the king seemed almost sorry to go.

'After an unpromising start,' he said, 'that was one of the most theatrical witch trials I've ever seen.'

'*Theatrical?*' Maira caught my eye.

'Indeed.' He stared into the middle distance. 'In the words of our wonderful playwright, all the world is a stage, and all the men and women merely players.'

Maira spluttered. Bea crammed her fingers into her mouth and pulled a face. Jem walked away.

I was glad, of all of us, it was Ellis who'd chosen to be a player on the world's stage. Though I'd a strong suspicion this wasn't what the king meant; a part of him still seemed to believe that witch trials and entertainment were more or less the same thing.

VI

IN WHICH FORTUNE DISCOVERS WHERE SHE BELONGS

33

For any sensible person, that would've been it: enough adventure, enough danger, enough of the sea to last a lifetime. And when I first returned home to Fair Maidens Lane, I did feel that way. Around our house, our church, our chicken shed, the floodwater was still ankle-deep, and pooled muddily in the lane from the crossroads. Our hamlet had become a little island, a haven from the world. We were maidens who could look after ourselves, and wanted to be left alone to do so. The king's absolution helped with that: nowadays our landowning neighbours kept a respectful distance.

Every day I expected Susannah and Bea to take off in search of Ellis. Now she knew he'd survived I was sure she'd want to be reunited, and I wanted that for them too, though I'd be heartbroken to lose them. Yet when I got up the courage to ask, all Susannah said was,

'He's happy, and so am I. I'll find him one day, when he wants to be found.'

*

One fine spring evening, Maira came calling just as we were sitting down to eat. Jem pulled up an extra chair, Abigail stared with her mouth open, and Mother insisted she stay for one of her special meat pies.

'We are sailing from Withy Cove in a couple of weeks,' Maira explained. 'The boat repairs took longer than we thought. And we can't move it, either. Seems we have need of your horse after all.'

It felt like a lifetime ago that she'd asked me to join her crew. Now, with her sitting at our supper table, the appeal of it began to nudge at me again.

'May we borrow Blaze to pull the boat down to the sea?' she asked. 'She's a big strong brute, isn't she?'

'She is,' Susannah agreed. 'And you'd be welcome to her, if that's all right with everyone?'

We all said it was.

'You'll need Susannah too, then. That horse dotes on her,' Jem said proudly.

And I was pretty sure he *winked* at Susannah, though it was hard to be certain with Mother and

Abigail moving between us as they handed out plates of pie and spring greens.

'And how are you, Fortune, the girl who doesn't drown?' Maira asked.

With all eyes were on me, I felt myself redden.

'Thanks to Jem,' I said. 'He's the one who pulled me out.'

'Hmmm. I'm sure the caul played a part in it too.'

Abigail took her seat. 'What caul?'

Maira chewed for a moment, head on one side, then gestured at Abigail with her knife. 'Do you know Fortune's blessed?'

'Blessed?' My sister laughed. 'What, old fleabag here?'

I scowled at her, but Maira convinced her it was true. 'And,' she pointed out, 'when the person's in danger, their caul becomes wet. That's what happened with yours, Fortune.'

She explained how Jem had come running across the meadow with news of my arrest. At first he'd been so shaken and breathless they'd had trouble understanding what had happened – and he was sweating too, all down his left side. Then, in my jacket pocket, they'd discovered the caul, so wet it had soaked through into his shirt.

'We'd swapped clothes at the town hall, hadn't we?' Jem reminded me.

It was a lot to think about. Susannah and her sewing, my caul: both had been signs that bad things were going to happen, and much as I'd wanted to play them down, they had proved to be right. Bad things *did* happen.

'I still don't think that makes any of us witches,' I pointed out.

'Witches are simply strong women, that's what you once told me,' said Susannah. 'You said everyone has a little strangeness in them, and that some things just can't be explained.'

'Some of us more than others,' Jem said, giving me a pointed look. 'No wonder you love the sea so much, sister. And I didn't, not at first.'

Maira laughed. Then, shovelling the last of her pie into her mouth, she stood up. With her long hair tucked inside her coat collar, she could easily have been mistaken for a handsome boy.

'Thank you for supper,' she said, making for the door.

Before I could stop myself, I blurted out, 'Can't I come with you?'

'Fortune!' Jem looked horrified.

'But I think maybe I'd like to,' I confessed. A table of

stunned faces stared back at me. 'Maira asked me to join her ship a while ago, and I've given it some thought.'

Maira sighed, twirling her hat in her hands. 'Give it some more thought, then. You've been through a lot, Fortune. You need time to heal and recover.'

'But I'm fine,' I protested.

Mother squeezed my shoulder gently. 'She's right, love. Give yourself a little time.'

'Come by with the horse in a couple of weeks when you've rested,' Maira said. 'Bring Susannah and Jem too. If you're not fit to sail, I might have something to offer them.'

*

Once she'd gone, I huffed a bit to Jem. 'If I can't go then you're *certainly* not. That wouldn't be fair.'

'Don't worry,' Jem insisted. 'You won't get me on a boat again, not in a hundred years.'

I told him he was a sparrow-brain. He flicked my ear. Of all the challenges being a sailor would bring, leaving him would be the hardest.

*

Soon after this, Susannah and I struck a deal: she'd take Ellen's gowns back to Glastonbury – I still couldn't face the place – if I'd teach her to swim. So twice a day, in the mild spring sunshine, we trooped down to the beach. Jem tagged along, insisting he'd look after Bea, who was now taking her first wobbly steps. I wasn't fooled. Since that time at the supper table, he and Susannah had been sharing quite a few *looks*. It was no surprise that Abigail had noticed too.

'I wish they didn't have to be so soppy,' I muttered as we watched them feeding the chickens together one morning. 'Doesn't it make you feel slightly sick?'

'I think it's lovely.' Abigail sighed. 'Jem deserves a good wife.'

'*Wife?*' I was reminded of what I'd thought of Susannah when I first met her – neat, demure, quiet.

'Don't be fooled by what she looks like,' I said. 'There are lots of ways to be a strong woman – Susannah's taught me that. It's not all about breeches, you know.'

Abigail laughed.

*

Meanwhile, we kept up with the swimming lessons. The first time I'd gone down to my beloved beach, I'd been horrified to see the damage that the floods had caused. Boulders that'd once lain down at the tideline were now strewn across the fields like toadstools. The gentle curve of the cliff looked jagged, bitten away at, and the slope of the shingle was so steep we almost had to scramble on our backsides to reach the water's edge.

Susannah was a very fast learner. Within days of living with us she could build a decent fire, bake bread, catch a chicken for the pot. The swimming took longer to master. She still didn't entirely trust the sea, and for that I didn't blame her: it had turned our lives upside down.

After a fair bit of splashing and spluttering, and telling me to stop being so strict, the day arrived when Susannah swam her first few strokes. It was the perfect doggy-paddle, and the delight on her face was priceless.

'Watch me again, Fortune!' she cried.

Jem ran home to fetch Mother and Abigail so they could see for themselves. By the time he returned with them, Susannah was swimming on her back and laughing. Mother, who'd taken to Susannah like another daughter, pushed a stray lock of hair off my face.

'You're a special one, Fortune, you know that, don't you?' she said.

I blinked, smiled, felt suddenly warm. But I also knew how fine the line was between 'special' and 'strange'. One person's beloved daughter could be another person's witch, and fear made people's attitudes change in the blink of an eye. Even the king himself didn't seem to understand it. We did, and we wouldn't ever forget it.

34

With every passing day the water dropped further, until the last of it was swept out of our yard and everything began to dry out. There were changes – little ones at first, like putting chairs back in different places or deciding the kitchen was better without rush matting on the floor. Abigail climbed the church roof and took in the prayer books. Those crispy, crinkled pages would serve as a reminder, people said, of things mankind couldn't control.

Then new people moved in to Old Margaret's cottage. They were a family called the Fitzpatricks, whose home on the outskirts of town had been flattened by the flood. There were ten of them, a mother and father and eight children. Overnight our little hamlet doubled in size. Jem wasn't the only young man any more, which I think made him relieved. It also gave Abigail something new to gossip about, although judging by her daft behaviour around the Fitzpatricks' eldest son, Tom, the talk would soon be about her.

*

On the first Tuesday of Lent, we took Blaze and as many ropes as we could muster to Withy Cove. It was a bright, breezy day, the snowdrops going over and primroses beginning to take their place. The time I'd taken to rest and recover had only strengthened my desire to go to sea. Now, at last, that day had arrived and I'd made up my mind. If Maira would have me, I was going. My family and friends still weren't overly keen, but they were kind enough not to stand in my way.

In the sack over my shoulder was my one clean shirt, a small pebble from our beach, and Mother's lucky little parcel. Jem was on one side of me, whistling. On the other, Susannah and Bea. I felt, in that moment, complete.

An awful lot had happened since I'd last seen the *Songbird*. The sight of it, lying on its side in the meadow, made me feel a bit overwhelmed.

'That's a small boat,' Jem muttered to me. 'You're not really crossing the ocean in it, are you?'

I was thinking the same. In my mind's eye the

Songbird had been a decent-sized vessel, but in reality, it was little more than a fishing rig.

'There's plenty of space on board,' I replied, not wanting him to see I was worried.

*

With the help of Maira and her crew, we tied Blaze to the boat. She had the look of a horse who'd really rather be eating grass. But on the count of three, Susannah clicked her tongue and led her forward, while the rest of us pushed from the back.

It was a bumpy, stop-start sort of journey. A couple of ropes came undone, and when the ground got wetter nearer the sea, we had to tie sacks to Blaze's feet so she could get proper purchase on the grass. In less than an hour, we hit the shingle of the cove. Another almighty heave, a bit of splashing and snorting from Blaze, and the boat slipped into the water. A huge cheer went up.

'That's the girl!' Susannah cried, clapping Blaze's sweaty neck with pride.

All too quickly, Maira's crew climbed on board, readying themselves for the journey ahead. There was a deck to clean, supplies to check, maps to read. And I knew that if I was joining them, now was the time to say my goodbyes.

Mother, who was already brimming with tears, said she'd go on home with Abigail and Blaze. As we parted, she held my face between her hands.

'Do better than your father did,' she said. 'Make sure you come back to us.'

'I will,' I promised. 'I'll bring home a purse this time, and all.'

Then it was Abigail's turn.

'Sorry for not always understanding you and your clothes,' she said, looking surprisingly contrite.

I shrugged, smiled. Most of what I'd worn these past weeks had belonged to someone else.

'I mean it, Fortune,' she said, with force. 'People have tried to crush you and make you into a person that you're not. You've stayed true to who you want to be, and that takes courage.'

I glanced down at my leggings and boots. If I'd looked at her I'd have started crying.

With just Jem, Susannah and Bea remaining now, we all went down to the water's edge. Maira was on deck, checking what seemed to be a map as two of the crew unfurled the boat's mainsail – actually, I noticed now, its only sail.

'Don't say a word,' I muttered to Jem.

From up on deck, Pepper was waving to us. 'Come up! All of you! Come and have a look!'

Flint and Pepper heaved me on to the boat. Before he could object, they did the same with Jem, despite him muttering that he wasn't staying.

'Any room for us?' Susannah asked.

Within moments, they were on board too. Pepper, taking Bea from Susannah, started showing her the ropes and mast like she was his favourite little sister.

'She can walk now,' Susannah told him, 'though she'll need to hold your hand.'

Soon little Bea was stomping up and down like she owned the place, though it wasn't a big deck. Ropes and buckets lay heaped at its edges, and with all of us on board, there was no denying how crowded it was.

'Well.' Maira, tipping back her cap, eyed me up and down with a smile. 'Someone's looking recovered.'

I took a deep breath, trying to calm my excitement. 'I am.'

She patted the top of my arm, just once. 'And the caul?'

'In my bag with my things.'

'Good. Keep it safe. Keep *us* safe.'

'Where are we headed?' I asked.

She pointed straight out over the water. 'There, to start with.'

We'd been so busy this last hour, I'd barely looked up long enough to notice the other vessel moored just outside of the bay. It was huge, easily one hundred feet long, with three masts and a beautiful wooden hull. Already there were crew on board, climbing the rigging, scrubbing the decks, though from this distance they were as small as ants.

'Goodness!' I breathed. 'That's our *ship*?'

'Indeed,' Maira replied, matter-of-fact. 'The *Pride of Bristol*. She's taking us and a hull full of grain to Jamaica.'

I'd never been to Bristol, let alone this place called Jamaica. Just the name sounded magical, like silver trickling off Maira's tongue. There was so much I wanted to ask, but I swallowed my questions because Flint was raising our anchor.

'You'd better go if you're going,' I said to Jem, a lump already in my throat.

Yet he was struggling to peel his eyes away from the big ship.

'You're welcome to join us, Jem. We're always in need of trustworthy crew,' Maira offered.

He glanced at me, at Susannah and at Bea, who was refusing to let go of Pepper's hand.

'She wants to stay!' Susannah laughed.

'Well, we could, if Maira meant what she said about having work to offer us,' Jem replied.

Susannah, catching the seriousness of his tone, stopped laughing.

'Could we?' she said, her eyes wide. 'Oh, Maira, *could* we?'

Maira hesitated. For a moment, I was sure she was going to say no. But I think she saw the strength in Susannah. Here was someone who wasn't just courageous and clever, but had heart enough to love her baby sister. And, so it seemed, my brother Jem.

'I must be mad,' Maira said, laughing, shaking her head. 'I must be truly mad.'

*

Late afternoon we set sail for Jamaica. 'The breeze was a gentle southerly, the sea calm, visibility good.' These were the words Maira read aloud to us from her logbook: to me they sounded like a spell.

As we travelled down the Bristol Channel we passed the little brown-sand beach of Fair Maidens Lane. To think of all the days I'd stood on that shore, wishing for something I couldn't even name. On the hillside above, a small herd of recently purchased cows were grazing, and further inland someone's laundry lay spread over bushes to dry in the sun. We watched it all go by and yet it didn't feel like I was saying farewell to somewhere dear, because I'd finally found where I belonged.

*

Another wonderful thing happened later that day, as we passed the North Devon coast. It was dusk and the sun was melting colours into the sea. To our left, high up on the clifftop a great bonfire blazed. There were bright-patterned tents pitched in a ring around it, and as the breeze blew it carried music and voices out across the water. Drawn to the sounds, we rested our elbows on the side of the ship to listen.

'It's a festival, isn't it?' Jem asked.

'Think so,' I said.

Bea, who'd been dozing on Susannah's hip, suddenly threw her arms in the air and giggled.

'What's she seen?' Susannah wondered.

'Something on the shore, look!' I replied, and we all followed her gaze back to the ring of tents high up on the cliff.

In amongst the browns and greys of people in the crowd were odd spots of red, yellow, green – the costumes, I supposed, of the performers. One in particular caught my eye. A young man, by the looks of him, small and agile, wearing a bold purple and white striped tunic. The crowd were standing back to give him space. And no wonder. He was doing the best somersaults I'd ever witnessed.

'Can you see him?' Jem clapped his hands in delight. 'He's brilliant!'

'He is,' Susannah murmured, a smile spreading across her face. 'He really is.'

Bea, arms flung wide, kept laughing.

I didn't take my eyes off the acrobat. Even this far away, I knew in my bones that it was Ellis.

Quicker than any of us would've liked, we left the festival behind. I fell quiet and thoughtful, then, staring out over the molten-red water as the sun sank lower in the sky. Back at home, Mother and Abigail would be shutting up the chickens and bringing in the laundry. Or maybe my sister had wrapped up a slice of leftover pie and taken it round to Tom Fitzpatrick.

Times were changing. Life was changing.

Yet, it was us that were different now, not the sea. It was as it always was – cold, salty-sharp, tingling with possibilities. It didn't hate or judge or hunt down what it was scared of.

It simply was.

We'd travelled so far these past months, and another journey was just beginning. The stars were in the evening sky. Our ship sailed onwards.

AUTHOR'S NOTE

At approximately 9 a.m. on the morning of 29th January 1607, a catastrophic flood hit the coastline of Devon, Somerset, Gloucestershire and South Wales. Over two thousand people drowned: homes were lost, livestock swept away, the entire village of Brean in Somerset destroyed. Over two hundred square miles of land lay underwater. The sea travelled as far inland as Glastonbury Tor, some fourteen miles from the coast. At Kingston Seymour, near Bristol, the village church bears a mark which shows the flood reached twenty-five feet at its height.

Eyewitness accounts from the time describe the sea moving 'faster than a greyhound could run', of 'mighty hilles of water' and 'some fog or mist coming in with great swiftness'. It was these accounts, and the research they inspired, that formed the argument put forward in 2002 of the flood being a tsunami. Professor

Simon Haslett of Bath Spa University and Australian geologist Ted Bryant of the University of Wollongong found evidence of soil types, coastal erosion and boulder deposits all suggesting the water had travelled very quickly and with great force. Their research is the subject of a fascinating *Timewatch* documentary 'The Killer Wave' in 2005, which can still be viewed on YouTube.

For the benefit of my story, I have woven the tsunami theory alongside other seventeenth century narratives, namely those of superstition and witchcraft. The climate at this time was experiencing a cooling period known as the 'Little Ice Age', which meant extreme weather events – storms, droughts, cold winters, floods – were more frequent. It wasn't uncommon for such events to be seen as punishment from God, and that something – or someone – was to blame.

In 1604, harming another person by 'magic' became a crime punishable by death. Although witch-hunts in the UK weren't as widespread as in Europe, there were numerous accounts of witch trials in Somerset in the early 1600s. I found no evidence that King James I or the Essex-based witchfinder Matthew Hopkins visited Somerset during this time – that's my invention. Yet both men's views had a huge impact on how women

– particularly the old, the sick, the slightly odd – were perceived during the seventeenth century and beyond. So I've included them in my story: perhaps I've put them on trial. That's for you, the reader, to decide.

Q & A WITH EMMA CARROLL

You are so good at making readers feel like they are experiencing first-hand the period of history that you are writing about. What inspired this setting and how did you go about creating the backdrop to the events of this book?

Somerset is my home, I was born and raised here, so I get a lot of my inspiration from the landscape and local history. The places affected by the 1607 flood are all known to me. What I also needed was a personal narrative to run alongside that of the flood, and when I delved into the Jacobean era, fears of witchcraft and the growing trade in sugar were two things that leaped out at me. So I decided to weave these in to Fortune's story.

Fortune is hired to tend to Ellis to make him more 'manly'; women thriving by themselves

are seen to be a nuisance and in need of a man to take charge; and if women are right about their intuition, they are quickly accused of being a witch. Did you consciously set out to challenge gender stereotypes when writing this book?

I hope all my stories explore gender in some way. We live in a world where, even now, gender roles are constantly challenged – in the workplace, in the media, by politicians. I'm all for people and personalities rather than narrowing things down to boy/girl characters. The early seventeenth century is particularly vivid and violent example of what happens when gender roles are enforced to the extreme.

What are the main messages you would like readers to take from this story?

That we're all individuals with our own quirks and characters, and should embrace our differences, not try to hide or change them.

What did you edit out of this book and why?

Originally, the story started at the trial. There was

another Sharpe sister called Eleanor who was rather duplicitous. She over-complicated the plot so had to go!

Can you talk us through the transformation of Fortune throughout the story, her character development and growth?

We first meet Fortune as a noisy, reckless girl who thinks of life as one big adventure. When events at home take a sinister turn, she's forced to grow up fast and make her own way in the world. Despite feeling overwhelmed and constantly out of place, she finds friendship and courage where she least expects it, and learns that appearances can be deceptive.

How important are your characters' names? How do you go about creating them?

Naming characters is one of my favourite parts to writing a story. For ideas, I'll look up birth registers for the year characters would've been born, so their names feel appropriate to the era. Sometimes a name will just land in my head, sometimes it'll come from research. Fortune, Susannah and Ellis are all early seventeenth century names. Occasionally, I'll be inspired by a real name: Dr Blood is named after my own childhood dentist, who was brilliant – and female – so nothing at all like the character in this book!

Family and relationships are often a focus in your stories. Do you ever see yourself or your family in any of your characters? And if you had to pick one character that is most like you from your books, who it would be and why?

Family and friends are hugely significant in my life, so yes, there are lots of echoes of my own experiences in the stories I write. Many of the names I use come from relatives – Tilly, Louie, Will, Cliff, Ephraim, are all named after my grandparents and great-grandparents. The character who is most like me is probably Tilly in *Frost Hollow Hall*!

Your books always have such a distinctive and authentic aesthetic about them. What do you feel that the cover artwork brings to your books?

Faber hit on an absolute super-talent when they asked Julian De Narvaez to illustrate my covers. His artwork so cleverly mixes the eerie with the nostalgic, so you feel as if you're about to read something old-fashioned, yet not quite traditional, which is exactly how I try to approach writing historical fiction. Julian's art, coupled with Faber's designers, makes those covers really arresting. They don't look like other book covers, somehow. As far as I know I'm the only UK author Julian does cover art for – and I love that!

If you could have lived through any period of history, which would it be and why?

I think the Victorian era would be fascinating, with so many new inventions and ideas whizzing about. Also the end of the eighteenth century because revolution was in the air.

Which books have been most influential to you throughout your writing career?

I grew up on a diet of pony books, ghost stories and the Moomins. As an adult, I became hooked on historical fiction in my twenties after reading *Fingersmith* by Sarah Waters. I'm also a huge Daphne Du Maurier fan. Both these writers have a very strong sense of place in their writing, and an undercurrent of something unsettling going on, which I love.

What does a day in the life of Emma Carroll look like when you're writing?

I've recently discovered I write better later in the day, which isn't just an excuse for a lie-in, honest! A writing day for me consists of getting up, walking my dogs, doing a couple of hours writing at my desk, then lunch, then writing downstairs on the sofa, surrounded by dogs. I tend to find the first 30k of an early draft the hardest part. My favourite part of the process is editing, because this is when the story thickens up and I can weave in the layers.

As a former teacher yourself, what advice would you give to teachers about how to develop reading for pleasure – especially historical fiction – in their schools?

Make sure your school has a skilled librarian and a proper library. Model reading to your pupils: the best reading practice I've seen is where the teachers are massively enthusiastic about kids' books, both old and new. Approach historical fiction story first. This is how I do it as a writer. The adventure, the characters, always come first. The history part of things is world-building, just as it would be in a fantasy novel.

What advice would you give to any budding young authors?

Read, read, read. All writers are passionate readers. It's where a lot of inspiration comes from, and where we learn how to craft a story. Also, getting it right takes time. Be patient and let your story grow.

Things to Talk About

* Old Margaret is taken away and accused of witchcraft. Do you believe that witchcraft existed?

* The hamlet of Fair Maidens Lane put a man in charge, due to men saying that the women couldn't thrive by themselves. Think about women who are in powerful positions in the world today. What skills do they have?

* Fortune's mother encouraged her to pretend she was a boy so she could get a job more easily. Does the power of the world today still lie in the hands of men or are things more balanced?

* Do you think there are certain circumstances

where it is acceptable for children to work or should they be in school?

* Fortune is employed by Mr Spicer at the hiring fair in order to make his son 'more manly'. What do you think he meant by this?

* In the story, certain activities are considered suitable only for boys or girls. What do you think about this?

* Mr Spicer tries to hide his youngest daughter Bea away after his wife died in childbirth. Why do you think he did this?

* There is a big gap between the rich and the poor in this book. Do you think that only the rich people should be the ones making the decisions with the power in life just because they have lots of money?

* Fortune says: 'But doesn't everyone have a bit of strangeness in them?' Is this true? If so, what is your bit of strangeness?

* There is a popular saying that 'knowledge is power'. What does this mean? Why do you think some people afraid of knowledge?

* Travelling theatre troupes were a common form of entertainment at the time of the story. Can you think of anything similar that happens today? How has our entertainment changed over the years?

With thanks to Scott Evans (The Reader Teacher & #PrimarySchoolBookClub) for writing these questions and discussion points.

For more resources, head to:
www.faber.co.uk/faber-childrens-resources

Tell us what you think!
🐦 **@FaberChildrens #SomersetTsunami**